FROM THE WORLD OF

Also by Derek Landy:

DEREK LANDY

HarperCollins *Children's Books*

First published in hardback in Great Britain by HarperCollins *Children's Books* 2013
HarperCollins *Children's Books* is a division of
HarperCollins*Publishers* Ltd
77-85 Fulham Palace Road, Hammersmith, London W6 8JB

Visit us on the web at www.harpercollins.co.uk

Visit Skulduggery Pleasant at
www.skulduggerypleasant.co.uk

Derek Landy blogs under duress at
www.dereklandy.blogspot.com

4

Illuminated letters © Tom Percival 2012
Skulduggery Pleasant™ Derek Landy
SP Logo™ HarperCollins*Publishers*

HB ISBN: 978-0-00-750092-5
TPB ISBN: 978-0-00-751237-9

Typeset in Baskerville MT by Palimpsest Book Production Limited,
Falkirk, Stirlingshire

Printed and bound in England by
Clays Ltd, St Ives plc

MIX
Paper from
responsible sources
FSC
www.fsc.org
FSC® C007454

FSC™ is a non-profit international organisation established to promote
the responsible management of the world's forests. Products carrying the
FSC label are independently certified to assure consumers that they come
from forests that are managed to meet the social, economic and
ecological needs of present and future generations,
and other controlled sources.

Find out more about HarperCollins and the environment at
www.harpercollins.co.uk/green

This book is dedicated to Brendan Bourke.

I am brash, arrogant, egotistical and incredibly narcissistic. Brendan was none of these things. Brendan was nice, and modest, and friendly, and he didn't have one bitter bone in his body.

He was so completely weird.

He gave me my start as a writer and for that alone the world owes him an enormous debt of gratitude.

I may be the Greatest Writer Who Ever Lived™, I may be the Golden God, but Brendan? Brendan was the Golden God's *uncle*.

1

t had seemed like a good idea at the time, hiding out at her old place in London. Only an idiot would return to a known residence, she figured, and since she wasn't an idiot, it would naturally follow that they'd never think to look for her there. The fact that they'd been lying in wait offended her more than anything else.

Tanith sprinted across the rooftop, boots splashing through a puddle as big as a lake, and leaped off the edge. The lane whipped beneath her and the night air stung her eyes. She collided with the building on the other side and clung there for a moment, then got her feet against the bricks and ran on, sideways. She jumped a string of windows one at a time, got round the corner and crouched there to catch her breath.

She hadn't seen Sanguine escape, but he'd probably just slipped through the floor and burrowed away. Of course, there was the distinct possibility that they'd got to him before he could do that. If that had happened, he'd be dead by now. You didn't arrest someone like Billy-Ray Sanguine, she knew, someone who could escape from any cell and slip out of any restraint. You killed him when you had the chance. Tanith hoped he wasn't dead. He was useful to her.

She edged closer to the corner, had a peek round. The rooftops were clear. She'd lost them. Her hand, which had been gripping the hilt of her sword, relaxed, and she felt the reassuring weight of the blade return to its natural balance across her back. She straightened her legs and stood out from the wall, her blonde hair falling in front of her face as she looked at the cars passing below. The safest thing would be to get down to street level, hail a taxi or get the Tube. But in order to do that, she'd have to dump her sword. Her coat was still lying on the floor of her apartment. She loved that coat. When she wore it, it concealed the sword. She loved her coat, but she was *in* love with her sword. She could no more abandon it than any other woman could abandon her own arm.

She turned, walked up the wall, made sure no one was waiting for her, and climbed on to the roof. If poor old Billy-Ray was dead, she'd need to find someone to replace him, which wasn't going to be easy. He was a fully functional sociopath, which made him useful in all sorts of fun ways. And she had a plan. She needed him for her plan to succeed. It was a good plan, too. Sneaky. She was proud of it, and looked forward to seeing how it would work out. She really hoped Sanguine wasn't dead.

Tanith stopped moving. On the building opposite, a man stood. Dressed in grey, with a visored helmet and a scythe in his hands. He hadn't seen her yet. She stepped backwards, started to turn, saw movement out of the corner of her eye.

Another Cleaver, leaping at her, the blade of his scythe darkened with fire to stop it glinting in the streetlights.

Tanith threw herself back, felt the scythe whisper past her throat. The Cleaver landed and came forward and she rolled and got up, her sword clearing its sheath. She met the next swipe and kicked, but he twisted his body out of the way as he spun the scythe so that the long handle cracked against her head. Cursing, Tanith stumbled, swung wildly with her sword to keep him back. The scythe handle hit her knee and she howled, and barely managed to fend off the blow that would have separated her pretty head from her pretty body.

The other Cleaver jumped across the chasm between the buildings, his legs tucked under him. Tanith wished she were an

Elemental, so she could send a gust of wind to throw him back, let him fall to his death. But she wasn't, and he landed, and now she had two Cleavers to deal with.

There was a time when they'd been on the same side, but that was back before the Remnant had squirmed its way into her soul. That dark little creature had taken her conscience, ripped it away from her, but in its place she had been given so many extraordinary gifts, as twisted as they were terrible. One of these gifts was a brand-new purpose, and this purpose meant that she could not allow these Cleavers to beat her here, tonight, on this rooftop. Darquesse depended on her.

They closed in. Tanith could see her own reflection in their visors. Her lips were black, and black veins riddled her face, the only outward signs that she had a Remnant inside her. She bared her teeth in a crazy-woman smile and said, "Come and have a go if you think you're hard enough."

They definitely thought they were hard enough, and they came in strong and fast. Tanith didn't even have time to curse as she rolled and spun and defended. As her blade clashed with theirs, she started to wonder if she needed a new battle cry, something that wasn't so goading. *I like your shoes*, perhaps.

She dipped to the side and ran her sword across the first Cleaver's arm. She drew blood, but not a lot. Their uniforms were reinforced against attacks, both physical and magical. Unlike *her* outfit – boots and brown leather trousers and a nifty little waistcoat. She backed up, defending without thinking, letting her instincts control her arms, letting her legs go where they wanted. Her body was her survival tool. It would do its job with no help from her, allowing her mind to plan and strategise and scheme. Tonight, though, with the crescent moon somewhere behind her and light pollution blinding her to the stars above, the only thought that ricocheted around her head was, *if you don't end this, you're going to die.*

Tanith waited for an opening and dropped her sword as she lunged forward, through the first Cleaver's guard. She hugged him, pressed her head into his shoulder so he couldn't headbutt, and forced him back. He used her own momentum against her in order to hip-throw her to the roof's surface, but she held on to him, landed on her feet and reversed the throw. His scythe clattered down as he spun over her hip, then it was his turn to throw her. Closer and closer they got to the edge, reversal after reversal, grappling all the while, trying to gain the upper hand as the edge grew nearer. Maybe the Cleaver expected her to throw him one final time, then immediately try to disentangle herself to stop him from pulling her over the side with him. Instead, she tightened her hold and kicked off, and they both went over.

The moment the Cleaver realised what was going on he let

go of her, flailed about, tried to grab something where there was nothing to grab. Tanith was already bringing her knees up, pressing her feet against his belly. She released her hold and kicked herself away from him. She twisted, grabbed the edge of the roof and swung up, leaving him to fall. He didn't scream on the way down, and she didn't hear a splat or a crash, but she heard tyres squealing and horns blaring.

One down.

She cartwheeled to the side to avoid the second Cleaver's attack. The curved blade came for her again and she slipped, recovered quickly, scrambled away, searching for her sword, her lovely sword. His boot smashed into her foot, taking both her legs from under her, and she hit the ground hard and gracelessly. She turned on to her back, froze as the Cleaver stood over her, scythe centimetres from her throat. Her chest rose and fell quickly. The Cleaver wasn't even out of breath. Her body sucked the black veins down out of sight, sucked the blackness from her lips. She looked up at him, her face flushed but clear.

"OK," she said, "I surrender."

The Cleaver didn't respond. She didn't expect him to. He adjusted his grip on the scythe, preparing to ram it down. Her hands flew up, grabbed the staff just above the blade, held it at bay. He pushed down and she pushed back. Her muscles stood out, her biceps and triceps, tendons working like thin cables beneath the skin of her forearms. She had been strong when she'd been Tanith Low, Adept sorcerer and all-round good girl. Now that she was Tanith Low, Adept sorcerer and Remnant host, she was even stronger. But it didn't seem to be doing her much good against the blade that was steadily dropping towards her carotid artery.

In order to kick out she'd need to move her hips, which would weaken her hold, which would kill her. In order to force the blade to one side she'd need to move it off her centre line, which would weaken her hold, which would kill her. The more she thought about it, the longer the list grew of the things that would end up killing her.

Her eyes focused on where the blade met the staff, at the tight screw that held the scythe together. With breath hissing through her clenched teeth, Tanith moved her left hand down slowly, until she could feel the screw beneath her palm. She concentrated on it, the same way she would with a door, feeling the tumblers within the lock, moving them, getting them where she wanted them to be. It was the same principle. She was opening something that had been locked to her. She felt the screw turning. She felt it pressing into her palm.

The screw came away and Tanith pulled the scythe apart, taking the blade into her left hand and letting the tip of the staff hit the roof's surface by her right ear. She swiped, the blade cutting through the Cleaver's leg, and he fell back as she got up. He reached for her, but she used the blade to bat his hand away. The tips of his fingers fell like confetti. With her next swing, she took his head off, and his body crumpled. She heard the sound his helmet made as it rolled away, and she looked over just as it disappeared off the edge of the building. A few seconds later she heard it smash through someone's windscreen, and a horrified scream drifted up from the street.

She made sure no one else was about to jump out at her, then she dropped the scythe blade and walked over to her sword, returned it to its sheath. Then she went to look for Sanguine.

2

anguine had returned to the apartment to grab Tanith's coat – he knew how much she loved it – and on the way back he'd snagged himself a prisoner. The man whimpered and cried a little, but otherwise didn't do a whole lot, especially when Sanguine's straight razor pressed against his throat. Beyond them, where the alley met the brightly lit street, a sorcerer called Clagge hurried by, talking into his phone, doing his best to co-ordinate the hunt from ground level. Sanguine would have loved nothing more than to step out after him and snap his scrawny neck, were it not for the fact that the street was probably filled with sorcerers and plain-clothed

Cleavers. The sorcerer he had now, this whimpering little pipsqueak, was not integral to the Sanctuary operation, which was the only reason Sanguine hadn't killed him yet. That, and he'd probably work adequately well as a human shield, should the need arise.

Sanguine moved back, away from the street, taking his captive with him. "What's your name?" he asked.

"Please don't kill me," the man blurted.

"You mind if I call you Jethro? You don't particularly *look* like a Jethro, but I knew a fella who had that name, back in Texas. Ever been to Texas, Jethro?"

"No, I... I haven't."

"I'm from East Texas myself, but Jethro, the other Jethro, he was a West Texas boy. It's drier there. I prefer the east, around Nacogdoches. Ever heard of Nacogdoches?"

"No."

"Well, no matter. Point is, I'm calling you Jethro on account of how I once held this self-same blade to the throat of the first Jethro, the other Jethro, and he sounded an awful lot like you do now. Like he was scared I was gonna start cutting. Know what happened to him, Jethro?"

"You... you let him go?"

Sanguine chuckled. "I like you, boy. You got optimism in those bones. I like you so much that I ain't gonna tell you what

16

I did to poor old Jethro, the first Jethro, may he rest in peace, may they someday find his head. I'm gonna let you hold on to that little sliver of hope you got burning inside you, that I let him go, that he lived out the rest of his life in happiness and harmony."

"Th-thank you..."

"He'd have to live it out without his head though, which wouldn't be the easiest thing to do, but I'm gonna leave that little story open-ended for you. Because I like you. Because I want you to think you might survive this, as laughable as that seems. This your first time out, is it?"

"Sorry?"

"Out in the field, boy. You don't seem like the battle-hardened type to me."

"No," Jethro said, "I'm not. I... I usually sit behind a desk all day."

"Been passed over for promotion a few times, that it? Finally figured you ought to be climbing that corporate ladder, taking on a position of authority in the Sanctuary – would I be about right?"

"Yes. Yes, you would."

"So you requested this assignment, did you? Figured with that many agents and Cleavers around, you'd never even have to get close to the action. Right?"

"Right," he said, and sobbed.

"You figured hey, it's only two people. Only two fugitives we have to apprehend, and you wouldn't have to actually do anything, but it'd still be down on your record, yeah? You'd still be part of it. You'd still share in the glory."

"Please don't kill me, Mr Sanguine."

"Don't ruin the ending," Sanguine snarled, and threw Jethro against the wall. Jethro covered up, expecting an attack. Instead, Sanguine just stood there.

"What do you do in the Sanctuary?" he asked.

"Different things," Jethro answered, keeping his eyes down. "Administrative work. Nothing glamorous or... dangerous."

"You know what I heard? I heard all you guys were planning on declaring war on the Irish Sanctuary, that's what I heard. I heard the English Council and the German Council and the Americans and the French and most everyone else was planning on going in there and taking over."

"I wouldn't... I wouldn't know anything about that."

"No? Pity. It'd have been something to talk about to delay the inevitable."

Jethro swallowed thickly. "Inevitable?"

Sanguine nudged his sunglasses further up on the bridge of his nose. "Seems to be an awful lot of activity around here lately, and not just cos of us. Wanna tell me what's going on?"

"I... I don't know."

"Just to inform you, lying right now would not be the best move you could possibly make."

Jethro hesitated. "There's a... It's..."

Sanguine gave a little sigh. "Let me make it easy on you. It's something to do with a prisoner, isn't it?"

Jethro nodded. "An escaped prisoner."

"Why, that just happens to be one of my favourite kind. The escaped prisoner in question wouldn't happen to be Springheeled Jack, now would it?"

"You... you know?"

"Of course we know. Why d'you think we're in town? Now, a guy like you, Jethro, an up-and-comer, if you will, he'd be inclined to keep abreast of developments in the search for said escaped prisoner, now wouldn't he?"

"He would. I mean, I would. Yes. Please don't kill me."

"Let's not get ahead of ourselves. Jack's on the run, and you folk are closing in on him. I wanna know where the search is being concentrated. And don't bother lying. As you can see, some facts I already know, so you better be sticking to them 'less you want me in a bad mood."

Jethro swallowed, and did his best to stand a little straighter. "Let me go. You let me go and then I'll tell you. You can't... you can't threaten me. I have the information you want and... and you're not going to kill me before I tell you. You're just trying to scare me."

"People scare better when they're dying."

Jethro stopped trying to stand straight. "The East End," he croaked. "Spitalfields. We have it closed off. Nothing can get by the cordon without us knowing about it. He's trapped. He's got no way out."

Sanguine grinned. "Jethro, you have been a most helpful captive."

"Are you... are you going to let me live?"

Sanguine's grin grew wider. "Not even remotely."

With Jethro, the second Jethro, lying dead in the alley amid the junk and the debris of London, the ground cracked and crumbled beneath Sanguine's feet and he sank into the cold embrace of the earth. He moved down to absolute pitch-black, to a darkness no human eye could penetrate, and he watched the dirt and rock shift before him, the individual grains undulating in streams, like a school of fish, flowing round him and allowing him through.

He stopped for a moment, listening to the vibrations that spoke to him louder than any voice, then burrowed sideways. He slowed as the ground parted, opened for him like a door, and harsh light spilled in against his sunglasses. Sanguine had no eyes to hurt, and he stepped on to the train platform, feeling the wall close up behind him. The platform was almost empty, five people waiting there, not one of them having noticed his arrival.

The rumbling beneath his feet intensified, told him where the train was, how fast it was moving. Then he heard it approach, and moments later, he watched it appear, brakes whining as it slowed. The doors opened. People got off, people got on. Sanguine brushed a few flecks of dirt from his shoulder and slipped through the doors before they closed. The carriage was empty, and he sat.

He looked at the leather coat in his hands. He wasn't worried about Tanith. She'd get away. He knew she would. She'd probably led those Cleavers a merry dance, then disappeared, leaving them floundering, with only her mocking laugh to assure them she'd been there at all. He'd meet up with her soon enough and he'd give her back her coat, and they'd kiss, and he'd stroke her hair, and she'd tell him about all the Cleavers she'd killed. She was everything he'd always wanted in a woman. Beautiful, smart, tough, twisted.

Sure, she was utterly devoted to this Darquesse person, this woman that all the psychics had dreamed about, the one that was going to end the world. Tanith had glimpsed the future, and the Remnant part of her was looking forward to all the

21

devastation and destruction that was on the horizon. Was it healthy, loving someone who wanted to help end the world? He freely admitted that it probably wasn't. And he knew that there was *something* she wasn't telling him. Some little nugget of information she'd been holding back about who this Darquesse was or where she'd be coming from. He let that go. He didn't mind that. People have secrets, after all. He had secrets. But apart from all that, they were a match made in heaven. Soulmates. Partners in crime.

And when this little caper of hers was over, he was going to ask her to be his wife.

3

The steps leading down were stone, old and cold and cracked. The walls were tight on either side, and curved with the steps as they sank into darkness. The girl's parents didn't say much. Her father led the way, her mother came behind and the girl was in the middle. The air was sharp and chill and not a word was spoken. Her mother hadn't been able to look at her since they'd arrived at the docks. The girl didn't know what she'd done wrong.

When the steps had done enough sinking, they came to a floor, and it was as good a floor as any, she supposed. It was flat and solid and wide, even if it was just as cold and old as the steps had been, and the walls, and the low ceilings that kept the whole place from caving in around them. The girl didn't like being underground. Already she missed the sun.

Her father led them through a passage, turned right and walked on, then bore left and kept going. They walked on and on and turned one way or the other, and the girl quickly lost track of where they'd been. It was all sputtering torches in brackets, feeble flames in the gloom.

"Remain here," her father said once they'd come to an empty chamber. She did as she was told, as was her way, and watched her parents leave through another passage. Her father held himself upright and seemed suddenly so frail. Her mother didn't look back.

The girl stood in the darkness, and waited.

And then she waited some more.

Eventually, a man wandered in, dressed in threadbare robes and broken sandals.

"Hello," he said. Even with that one word, he didn't sound English. The girl had never met a foreign person before.

"Hello," she answered, and then added, "pleased to meet you," because that was what you said to strangers upon first making their acquaintance.

He stood there and looked at her, and the girl waited for him to say something else. It wouldn't have been right for her to speak. She was a child, and children had to wait for their elders to initiate a conversation. Her father had been very strict about that, and it was a lesson she'd learned well.

"Do you have questions?" the man asked in that strange accent that clipped every word.

"Yes. Thank you. Where am I, if I may ask?"

"You do not know?"

"I'm here with my parents. They—"

"Your parents are gone," said the man. "They went away and left you here. This is where you live now."

The girl shook her head. "They wouldn't leave me," she said.

"I assure you, they have."

"My apologies, but you're wrong. My parents would not leave me."

"They got back on the boat an hour ago. This is your home now."

He was lying. Why was he lying? The girl had inherited her manners from her father. From her mother, she had inherited other attributes. "Tell me where they are or they'll be very cross," she said, using a voice that brooked no argument. "My brother will come looking for me, too. My brother is big and strong and he'll pull off your arms if he thinks it would make me smile."

The man sat on a step. He had an ordinary face. Not handsome, but not ugly. Just a face, like a million others. His dark hair drew back from his temples and was flecked with grey. His nose was long, his eyes gentle and the corners of his mouth turned upwards. "Did they give you a name?" he asked. "They didn't? Nor a nickname? Well, that might get annoying in the next few years, but you'll pick a name for yourself sooner or later and then we'll have something to call you."

"I'm not staying here for the next few years," said the girl, firmly acknowledging that the time for manners was at an end. "I'm not staying here at all."

The man continued like he hadn't heard her. "My name is Quoneel. It's an old name from a dead language, but I took it for my own because of what it means, and what it meant, and it is my name now and it protects me. Do you know how names work?"

"Of course," she said. "I'm eight, not stupid."

"And you have magic I take it?"

"Lots," said the girl. "So tell me where my parents are or I'll burn you where you sit." She clicked her fingers and flames danced in her hand.

Quoneel gave her a smile. "You are indeed a fierce one, child. Your mother was right."

"Where is she?"

"Gone, as I have said. I have not lied to you. They have left you here, as they once left your brother."

The girl let the flames go out. "You know my brother?"

"I trained him. We all did. As we will train you. You will live here and train here and grow here, and when your Surge comes, you will leave as one of us."

"Who are you?"

"I am Quoneel."

"But what do you mean? Who will I be when I leave?"

"Who you will be, I do not know. But what you will be... If you survive, if you are as fierce as you seem, then you will be a hidden blade. Invisible. Untouchable. Unstoppable. You will be as quick and as strong as your brother, and as skilled and as deadly. Do you want that, little girl?"

It was as if he could see into her dreams, into her most private thoughts. She found herself nodding.

"Good," said Quoneel, and stood up. "Your training starts today."

They called her Highborn, the other children. They used it as a weapon to wound her. One of them, a girl with dull brown hair, but a sharp cruel tongue, was too vindictive to cross, so the others flocked to her side. The cruel girl was the first one of them to take a name, and she chose Avaunt.

Quoneel took the girl for a private lesson one day. "Do you know why they call you Highborn?" he asked.

"Because they don't like me," the girl said. The practice sword was heavy in her hands.

"And why don't they like you?"

"Because Avaunt doesn't like me."

"And why doesn't Avaunt like you?"

The girl shrugged, and attacked, and Quoneel stepped out of the way and struck her across the back of the knees.

"Avaunt doesn't like you because of the way you speak and the way you look and the way you walk."

The girl scowled and rubbed her legs. "That seems to be a lot of things."

"It does, doesn't it. You are well-spoken, and that points to breeding and education and privilege. You are pretty, and that means men and women will notice you. You walk with confidence, and that means people will know to

take you seriously. All of these are admirable qualities in a lady. But we do not train you to be a lady here. Attack."

The girl came forward again, careful not to fall into the same trap as last time. Instead, she fell into an altogether different trap, but one which was just as painful.

"We are the hidden blades, the knives in the shadows," said Quoneel. "We pass unnoticed amongst mortals and sorcerers alike. The privileged, the educated and the beautiful cannot do what we do. You must lose your bearing. You must lose your confidence. You must lose your poise."

His sword came at her head and she blocked, twisted, swung at him, but of course he was not standing where he had been a moment ago. He kicked her in the backside and she stumbled to the centre of the room.

"They call you Highborn because that is what will get you noticed," Quoneel told her. "You must learn to mumble your words, to shuffle your feet, to stoop your shoulders. Your eyes should be cast down in shame at all times. You are to be instantly forgettable. You are nothing to the mortals and the sorcerers. You are beneath them, unworthy of their attention."

"Yes, Master Quoneel."

"What are you waiting for? Attack."

And so she did.

4

The key to any successful heist was the team assembled to do the job. That was the first law of thievery. The second law, of course, was that thieves, by their very nature, were an untrustworthy lot – and if team members couldn't trust each other, then what was the point of being a team?

Tanith felt she had the answer. Sanguine wasn't so sure.

"This has been tried," he said. He was sitting at the small table in the small kitchen. "Me and my daddy tried it, got together a group of like-minded individuals and did our level best to kill everyone, yourself included. Correct me if I'm wrong, but you seem to be alive and kicking despite our best efforts."

Tanith stood by the window, mug of coffee in her hand. The safe house was drab and barely furnished, but at least they weren't going to be surprised by an army of Cleavers any time soon. "Your little Revengers' Club had a very basic flaw, though," she told him. "You all wanted the same thing."

"How was that a flaw? It brought everyone together, united for a common goal."

"And how long did they *stay* together? By the end of it, everyone was betraying everyone else, because you all wanted to be the one to kill Valkyrie or Skulduggery or Thurid Guild... Your little club unravelled, Billy-Ray. Having a common goal is not always a good thing."

"And you have the answer, I take it?"

She turned to him, smiling. He had his sunglasses off, and she looked into the dark holes where his eyes should have been. "Of course I do. The trick is to have everyone wanting something different – so that they're all taking part for their own unique reasons."

"Which means that we need to have something that each one of them wants."

"And what do you think I've been doing these past few weeks? I've been collecting our incentives. Really, Billy-Ray, you're just going to have to accept that I do know exactly what I'm doing."

He laughed. "Oh I believe you, darlin'. You've been proving

yourself to be quite the cunning little minx lately." He shrugged. "I'm behind you all the way, and you know it. So Springheeled Jack is the first team member to be recruited, is he?"

"No, actually. We're going to talk to an old friend of his first. Old friend of yours, too."

Sanguine's grin soured. "Aw, hell. Not him. You know he creeps me out."

"Dusk is a harmless little puppy once you get to know him."

"Dusk is a vampire. There ain't nothing harmless, little or puppyish about him."

Now it was Tanith's turn to shrug. "Then he'll be our rabid, bloodthirsty attack dog instead. Either way, he's getting a cuddle. Does someone else want a cuddle? Someone who is in this room with me right now?"

"I hope you don't think you can sway me from every argument with the promise of a cuddle."

Tanith put on a sad face, and turned back to the window. "Shame," she said.

A moment later she felt Sanguine's arms wrap round her. "Just this once," he said, and she laughed.

The vampires stood looking at the bones of the dinosaur and Dusk wondered what it would have been like to kill such a magnificent beast. Certainly it would have been more of a challenge than that posed by the mortals. He watched them hurry from exhibit to exhibit, either chasing after their squealing young or dragging them along behind, every sound they made amplified by the museum's cavernous halls.

"The boy?" asked Isara.

"Dead," said Dusk. "A year ago."

Isara nodded. Apart from that, she didn't move. No words slipped by her lips. No emotions slipped on to her face. Even her eyes were calm. But Dusk knew that inside her, twisting within her, were feelings alien to him. Love and loss and sorrow. The only feeling he could recognise was anger. And she had that, too.

"Did you kill him?" she asked.

"Of course not."

The ghost of a smile. "Of course not," she echoed. "You would not break the code, not even to punish one who had. How, then, did he die?"

"He had developed another unhealthy attachment to a girl," said Dusk, "but this one proved too much for him. She drowned him in salt water."

"Her name?"

"Does it matter?"

"I suppose not. The boy is dead, that's all I really care about. In its way, justice has been served. You must feel some satisfaction also."

He looked at her. "Must I?"

"Hrishi was your only friend in the world," said Isara, "and when you involved him in business that was not his own, the boy broke the code and took his head. Surely you feel some sense of responsibility for what happened?"

"No," said Dusk. "Hrishi knew the boy was young and impetuous and violent, and he still let his guard down. Hrishi paid for his foolishness."

"Be careful how you speak about him," Isara said, and looked at Dusk with fire and ice in her eyes. "It's your fault he died. You should have killed the boy when you found him."

"The code—"

"No one would have *known*. The boy was a danger to us all. He stalked and he tortured and he murdered every woman he became enamoured with. You should have killed him the instant you realised what he was. Hrishi's blood is on your hands."

"Perhaps."

"Do you even care?"

Dusk didn't see the point of stirring Isara's anger any further, so he stayed quiet. After a moment she turned, walked away, left him alone.

He looked at the dinosaur bones for a while longer, and then he too left the museum. The sun was warm on his skin as he walked. He got back to the house and found Tanith Low sitting on the cage in the living room, Billy-Ray Sanguine standing beside her.

"Nice place," Tanith said. "I have to admit, I didn't see you as the suburbanite type. I figured you'd be at home in a nice crypt somewhere, surrounded by candles and tapestries. The cage is a nice touch, though. Homey."

He'd heard what had happened, of course. He'd heard that a Remnant had taken up permanent residence inside Tanith's mind and body. But that still didn't mean he liked her.

"We're here to make you a proposition," said Sanguine.

"I'm not interested."

"We're putting a team together," said Tanith.

"It's been tried. It didn't work."

"We need your help."

"You can kill people without me."

"This isn't about killing anyone," Tanith said. "Quite the opposite, in fact. We want to save someone. We want to save Darquesse. A group of Elementals and Adepts has formed, a small team who are working on a way to stop her when she appears. Our aim is to stop *them* from stopping *her*."

"Why would I want to stop that? When she comes, she'll destroy the world."

"Not all of it," said Tanith. "Just the civilised part. And we're going to help her. Won't that be wonderful? She'll kill sorcerers and mortals and burn cities to cinders and sink entire continents into the sea, and you'll be free to hunt and kill the survivors. Doesn't that sound nice?"

"I don't care about any of this."

"We know you don't," Sanguine said, and nodded. "We know you're looking out for number one. And hey, buddy, I get that. I do. But we need you on our side. It's gonna be you, us, a few others... and Jack."

"Then I cannot be on your team. The last time I saw Springheeled Jack I was abandoning him to the Sanctuary authorities in Ireland."

"So you betrayed him," Tanith said. "So what? A little betrayal never hurt anyone. Listen, I know I can convince Jack to play nice. I have something he wants, after all. Just like I have something you want."

"And what is that?"

"Dusk, I look at you, and I see a soul without purpose. I mean, here you are, living in a very nice house with a time-locked cage where the couch should be. I don't know how you came to own this place – I'm sure the story is suitably entertaining – but you don't belong here. You've lost your focus."

"You think you can provide that focus?" Dusk asked. "I don't care about Darquesse. I don't care about anything."

"But that's a little bit of a lie, isn't it? See, Dusk, you do care about something. You care about one thing. You've always cared about this one thing, because you're a vampire – and this one thing plagues all vampires who were not turned willingly."

Dusk frowned.

"I know who turned you, Dusk."

"You're lying."

"No, I'm not. I know your story. Out walking one night, you were attacked; a nearby farmer came to your aid – he frightened off the beast... You recovered at his cottage, under the watchful eye of the farmer and his wife. And on the third night, you tore off your skin and devoured them. By then, of course, the one who had turned you was long gone."

"And how do *you* know who it was?"

"An Elemental was in the area around the time all of this was happening. He reported back to the Sanctuary like a good little operative, and in his report he mentioned the name of a vampire he had met. I know the name, Dusk. And I'll tell you – providing you help us."

"Tell me now."

"I'm not going to do that."

"How do I know you're telling the truth?"

"I try not to lie to vampires."

"Tell me who it was."

Tanith hopped down off the cage. "No. Here's the deal. You

help us. You get along with everyone else in the team, even Jack, and when it's over, I give you the name, and you go off and do whatever you want to do. Vampires hold grudges, don't they? I'd imagine you've been holding this grudge for a good long time."

"This might be it," said Sanguine. "This might be the one thing to make you break your precious little vampire code – never kill another one of your kind. What do you think, Dusk? Might this be what tips you over the edge?"

Dusk said nothing.

5

Rooftops and chimneys, that's all there was to see from up here. The whole thing reminded Sanguine of that scene from *Mary Poppins* where Dick Van Dyke starts dancing about with all those chimney sweeps high over London town. He wondered if Springheeled Jack ever took the time to dance about with chimney sweeps, singing as they went. Probably not, if he were being honest. Still, it was something to wonder as he waited there, whistling 'Chim Chim Cher-ee' and keeping watch for Cleavers.

Not even twenty minutes later, a long-fingered hand scuttled over the ledge like an unsettlingly ugly spider, followed by an arm and then a battered top hat with a lined, drawn, misshapen face beneath. Jack stayed down there, chin level with the roof, eyes on Sanguine.

"No one else here," Sanguine told him.

Jack's voice was high and strained. "'Cept for Cleavers," he said. "Cleavers're everywhere."

"Not here. Not right now. I've been here a whole half-hour and I haven't seen a single one."

"They're about."

"That I know. This whole area's one big search zone for them. But if you've got the skills, sneaking in and out isn't much of a problem. Come on up. We have time for a chat, don't we?"

Jack stayed put for a moment, and then with a grace so effortless it would have widened Sanguine's eyes had he not scooped them out long ago, he pulled himself up and stood there on the edge. His feet were bare, his clothes – top hat and tails – worn and musty.

"How'd you know where to find me?" Jack asked.

"I didn't," said Sanguine. "I reckoned you'd be keeping an eye out, though. Figured you'd find me if I waited long enough."

"What do you want?"

"To talk."

"That so? You're lookin' pretty calm for someone who should be worried."

"And why should I be worried? We're two old friends, standing on a rooftop, chatting."

"Last time I chatted to you, you had all these plans to set off the Desolation Engine, remember that? And then that sneaky vampire git turned and ran, left me to get pummelled and thrown in a cell."

Sanguine shrugged. "And how is that my fault? You know full well never to give a vampire good reason for revenge, and yet you still stopped him from killing Valkyrie Cain on that beach, four years ago."

"There were, what do you call them? Extenuatin' circumstances. You'd all lied to me."

"You can't take any of this personally, Jack."

"I can, and I do. It was because of Dusk, and because of you and your dear old dad, that I've been in a gaol cell for the last two years. I'd still be there right now if I hadn't escaped."

"Nonsense. We'd have come to get you out."

A sneer crossed Jack's face. "Not bloody likely."

"I'm serious. We were all set to mount a daring rescue attempt when we heard you'd managed it all on your own."

"And why would you want to get me out? Need my help, do you? Another dangerous little mission?"

"As a matter of fact, yes."

"Yeah, knew it. Get lost."

"Jack..."

"Not interested." Jack turned, knees bending, ready to leap away.

Sanguine stepped forward. "Where are you going? Where is there to go? They've got the area sealed off, Jack, and they're closing in. They're going to get you, drag you back and throw you in a cell so deep you'll never even *breathe* fresh air ever again."

"And let me guess," said Jack, turning his head slightly, "the alternative to all that is hookin' up with you and your dad and the vampire again, is it?"

"Not my dad. They have him locked away and no one knows where. As for Dusk, though, yeah, he's onboard."

"Forget it."

"Ask me who's leading this little mission."

"No."

"Tanith Low."

Jack turned fully now. "You what?"

"You've been out of the loop, Jack, so you won't have heard. She's got a Remnant inside her now. It's changed her outlook on a whole load of things. She's one of us."

"You bein' serious?"

"Would I joke about a woman who wears leather that tight?"

"Tanith Low's possessed by a shadowy little Remnant and has

gone all evil on us, has she?" Jack said, then considered it. "And what, exactly, would this mission entail?"

"It would entail, exactly, the retrieval of four God-Killer level weapons from around the world. We have all the locations – we just lack the manpower."

"And what'll you be usin' these weapons for, may I ask?"

"Well, that's a little bit of a secret at this juncture. If you sign on, though, everything will be explained."

Jack's eyes narrowed. "And the risk?"

"Apart from the resistance we'll face in the actual retrieval of the weapons from their current owners, there's also a little group of sorcerers who are going after the same things. Our aim is to get to the weapons first, swap them with some clever forgeries and slip out before anyone realises something is wrong."

"Who's in this little group of sorcerers?"

"Dexter Vex and a few others. Seven in all. Tanith's recruiting her own team to match it. You're our number-one pick."

"I won't be on any team with Dusk. If we leave him out, I'm in."

"That's great news. Tanith will be delighted. One slight problem. Dusk is already in."

"You said I was your number-one pick."

"And you are. In our hearts. Alphabetically, though, Dusk comes before you."

"And what do I get out of all this?"

"For a start, we burrow away from here and get you out of London and away from the search teams. If they do find you, you'll have our little group fighting by your side. But more than that – Tanith's been doing some research."

"Oh, yeah? About what?"

"About you, and what you are, and where you come from. If you help us find these weapons, she'll tell you everything you've always wanted to know."

"You're lyin'. She knows nothin' about any of that. No one does."

"Jack, you've been a killer all your life pretty much, right? You've been a villain. She's been a hero. She's had access to things you can only dream about."

"She knows what I am?"

"Yes, she does. Are you in?"

"Tex, if you're lying to me..."

"Jack, she needs her team. She's done her research. When this is over, you'll have your reward. So what do you say? Are you in?"

Jack raised a hand to his mouth, and his sharp little teeth worried the skin of his knuckle. It didn't, in fairness, take him all that long to think it over. "Yeah," he said. "I'm in."

"Wonderful news," Sanguine said, and smiled.

"So where is she? I can't wait to see the all-new, all-evil Tanith Low."

"You'll be seeing her soon enough, don't you worry. Right now she's recruiting the third member of our little group, someone who comes before both you and Dusk alphabetically, but a distant third in our hearts."

"Yeah?" Jack said. "And who might that be?"

Black Annis had had an ignominious end. There weren't many who could survive an encounter with her, not once she was mad and her skin was turning blue and her teeth were growing long and jagged. Her fingernails had silenced many a last scream and her jaws had clamped round many a throat. She was a people-eater, and had never seen anything wrong with that, and for most of her life she'd lived in one ditch or other, or a cave if she was lucky, its ground littered with the bones of her victims. Apart from one particular idiot who used to scurry around after her, no one who entered her lair had ever emerged.

Until the blonde. Until the blonde in the brown leather. And before Annis had known what the hell was happening, she was hog-tied and helpless and the blonde in the brown leather was smiling down at her.

Just like she was now.

Annis sat up in her narrow bed, in her cell that was far too cramped and far too bright. There was a toilet against one wall and a sink against another. She'd never needed a toilet or a sink when she was living in her ditch. That, she supposed, was the sole advantage of living in a ditch.

"Hi," said the blonde. She stood there in the open doorway, smiling, with that sword strapped to her back and all that brown leather barely keeping her in.

"You're looking well," said the blonde. Tanith Low, her name was. "Better than the last time I saw you, anyway. At least you're not wearing a sack."

Annis looked at her, but didn't move to get off the bed. "They starve me here."

"No, they don't. They feed you."

"I eat *people*. They don't give me people to eat. They give me animals. That's barbaric. At least people have a fighting chance to get away. The animals they give me are already dead. It's sickening, is what it is."

"Annis, you're a unique individual, which is why I'm here."

"I should rip your throat out."

"And if you could grow those sharp nails of yours, I'm sure that wouldn't be a problem for you. But you can't. You're stuck here in this little cell, your powers bound and your life drifting away from you. And let's face it, Annis, you're not getting any younger."

"Is that why you're here? To gloat?"

"Not at all. You see, the last time we met, I was the old me. But now I'm the new me, and the new me sees things differently from the old me. The new me would never have arrested you and dragged you from that ditch. And what a splendid ditch it was. Tell me something – did you like living in ditches?"

Annis glowered.

"I'm not trying to poke fun, honest I'm not. I don't think you did like living in ditches. I think it's just something you had to do because of your... condition." Tanith smiled gently. "What if I told you that I knew of a cure?"

Annis frowned. "Cure for what?"

"For what ails you. For your curse."

"A cure for my curse? There is no cure for my curse. I don't have a curse. I was born this way. This is natural."

"Annis, you don't know what you are, do you? You don't know why your skin turns blue or why your nails grow long and you don't know why you'd turn to stone if sunlight hit you."

"Yeah?" Annis said with a sniff. "And I suppose you do?"

"Actually, yes," Tanith said, "I do."

"You're lying."

"I have access to certain files and documents, and one of these files is about you. You were cursed, Annis. It's why you're the way you are. And there is a cure. But if you want it, you have to do something for me first."

46

"Like what?"

"I'm putting together a group of special individuals with unique talents, and I want you to be part of it."

"You want me to be in your gang? I eat people."

"The new me doesn't care," Tanith said. "Eat whomever you want. Apart from the other members of the team, obviously. That would be inconvenient. Just do what I say, and when our job is done, you'll be set free and you'll get the cure. The rest of your life is yours to live, however you want to live it. May I suggest not living it in a ditch?"

Annis stood. She wasn't a tall woman, so still had to look up. "You say you've changed. How do I know you're telling the truth?"

"Do you know what a Remnant is, Annis? I've got one of them inside me, permanently bonded to my soul. I'm a changed woman."

"So you'd be breaking me out of here, is that it?"

"That's it exactly. Providing you agree to my conditions."

Annis looked at her for a long while. "If you bust me out of here, you have a deal."

"Oh, good," Tanith said, grinning. "Come on."

She turned and walked out, and Annis hesitated. If this was some sort of trap, she couldn't see the point of it. So she followed.

"We're lucky," Tanith was saying as she walked. "They didn't put you in a top-security gaol. Don't get me wrong, Annis, you're a dangerous lady, you truly are. But prisons like these are designed to keep in prisoners who aren't really smart enough to try to escape."

Annis was barely listening. Her body tingled as her magic returned. It was such a wonderful feeling it almost took the breath from her. She could grow her fingernails and swipe that pretty blonde head from those pretty broad shoulders if she so wanted. But then what? She didn't know where the hell she was. She didn't know how the hell she'd get out.

They passed a man on the ground with his throat torn open. Another up ahead, and beside him, a woman. Annis's stomach rumbled.

"You kill all these?" she asked, salivating.

"Not all of them," said Tanith. "I have a friend with me. You'll meet him later. I think you'll like him. His name's Dusk. He's been cursed, too, in a way, so you'll probably have lots in common if you... oh, Annis, please. We really don't have time."

Annis looked up from where she was kneeling beside the dead sorcerer, but didn't answer. Even though she had a habit of living in ditches, she still didn't like to speak with her mouth full. Some things were just rude.

Sabine put the ring on the table, and watched Badstreet's eyes widen.

"Is that it?" he asked, his voice hushed. Around them, mortals laughed and joked and drank, and music played, and occasionally someone would nudge past Sabine on their way to the bar. Sabine didn't mind. The only thing she cared about was convincing the man before her that the metal band on the table was the Ring of Salumar.

"Yes, it is," she said. "Forged in shadow and fire by the seventh son of a seventh son, a blind man who spoke with the dead. He made that ring for the great sorcerer Salumar, but on the eve of delivery, the dead came to him, and told him Salumar was going to kill him. So he hid the ring, refused to hand it over and Salumar therefore killed him. A cautionary tale for those who don't believe that dead people can have a sense of humour. Pick it up."

Moving slowly, reverently, Badstreet did as she told him.

"It's heavy," he said. "And powerful. I can feel the magic, even holding it..."

He went to put it on, but Sabine's hand flashed, snatching the ring back. "Sorry," she grinned. "You break it, you buy it. You know how it is."

Badstreet's eyes narrowed. "You can't expect me to buy it without testing it."

"You don't need to test it," she laughed. "Badstreet, come on. A sorcerer of your ability doesn't need to slip the ring on to his finger to know the power it holds. You said so yourself, you could feel it."

He rubbed his hand along the stubble on his jawline. "It's like it's calling to me."

Sabine nodded, and did her best not to laugh. "Do you have the money?"

He hesitated, and she saw the debate going on behind his eyes. To pay, or not to pay, that was the question, and it was a debate Sabine was used to seeing. The outcome, of course, was never in question.

Badstreet passed an envelope to her beneath the table. Keeping it out of sight, Sabine opened it up and quickly counted. It certainly seemed to be all there. She nodded, pocketed the envelope, and put the ring into a small wooden box. Then she stood up, handed the box to Badstreet, and gave him her best smile.

"Pleasure doing business with you," she said.

She walked to the back of the pub, squeezing through the throngs of people. It would take Badstreet fifteen to twenty seconds to figure out how to open the box, another ten seconds of examining the ring and savouring the power, and then a full two to three minutes before the power started to fade and he was left with a useless trinket she'd picked up from a dingy shop on the way there. Plenty of time.

She had already deactivated the alarm, so she left quietly through the fire escape door, stepping into the alley behind the pub. She turned away from the street, because that would be the direction in which Badstreet would eventually sprint, and instead walked deeper into the darkness. Another job done. Another sucker suckered. All in a night's work.

"Such a naughty girl."

Sabine whirled, looked up. Standing straight out from the wall above her was a blonde woman in a long leather coat.

"Good to see some things haven't changed, though," the woman said, slowly strolling down to street level. "You were a sneaky little thief thirty years ago and you're a sneaky little thief now."

Sabine tried a smile. "Hi, Tanith. Been a while."

"It has at that," Tanith said, hopping to the ground. She was taller than Sabine. "To be honest, I never thought you'd live this long. Sneaky little Sabine, always conning the wrong people, always getting the wrong people mad with her. I thought you'd have ended up dead in the gutter a long time before this."

"Is that why you're here, then? To kill me?"

"Kill you?" Tanith laughed. "Now why would I do something as mean-spirited as that?"

"I heard you've got a Remnant inside you."

"True enough, but while my insides may be rotten, I still like a good reason to kill someone. It has to be either business, personal or out of sheer boredom. Do I look bored to you, Sabine?"

"So what do you want?"

Tanith's smile was as bright and radiant as ever. "You."

6

own there, in the dark and the cold, all the girl did was train.

In the mornings she trained her mind – languages and numbers and histories both known and hidden. She sat with the others in a semi-circle around the tutor, ignoring the whispers and the smirks and the laughs if ever she got a question wrong.

The afternoons were for training of a different sort. That was when they fought and climbed and ran and swam. That was when their muscles were stretched and torn and built up again, when their bodies were taught how to move independently of their minds. Muscle memory, the tutors called it. Making fighting second nature. Making killing an instinct.

The girl didn't like the idea of killing, even while she recognised it would have to be a necessary part of her training. The others claimed they didn't mind it. Avaunt even insisted she was looking forward to her first kill – then she'd always glance at the girl and everyone else would laugh. Avaunt kept up the act until the morning when she was called away by Quoneel.

When she returned, her robe was drenched in blood and her face was pale. Her eyes were wide and wet. The girl found her later, sobbing quietly in a dark corner. Avaunt looked up and called her Highborn again, called her worse names until the girl walked away and left her to her tears.

The girl wasn't looking forward to her first kill.

Quoneel took her out of lessons one day, and the girl followed dutifully after him, her belly in knots. They came to a small room where a woman was chained to a wall. She was the first person not dressed in robes that the girl had seen in a long, long time.

"Who are you?" the woman asked, frightened. Her hair was brown. She was slightly overweight. She looked the same age as the girl's own mother. "What do you want? If you let me go, I won't tell the police, I swear."

Quoneel handed the girl a dagger. "Kill her," he said.

The woman's eyes widened. The girl looked at the dagger.

"I can't," she said.

"But this is what you've been training for," said Quoneel. "When you are a hidden blade, you will claim many lives. This will be your first."

"But I don't even know this woman," said the girl.

"Your name," said Quoneel. "Loudly now, so the girl can hear."

"Tanith," said the woman. "Tanith Woodall. I have a son and daughter and they need me. Please. Please let me go back to them."

"There," said Quoneel. "Now you know her. Will taking her life be easier now?"

The girl shook her head. "She hasn't done anything to me. She hasn't hurt me. I can't just kill her."

"You can. It's quite easy."

"But why?"

"Because, as a hidden blade, you must kill those you are told to kill. And I am telling you to kill this woman."

Quoneel clicked his fingers and the chains holding the woman to the wall sprang open. The woman stumbled a little, rubbing her wrists, free but still terrified.

"Master, please..."

"I ask you, child, what use is a killer who cannot kill?"

The girl swallowed. "No use, Master."

"No use indeed. Since you joined us, you have been tested every day in every way. Every question we ask is a test. Every task you are given is a test. But none of those tests would end in your death were you to fail them. This is the first real test you've been given. Think carefully on how you wish to proceed."

"If... if I could just have a little more time," said the girl.

"To do what?"

"To prepare. To get myself ready."

"I see. So if we were to delay this test for six months or so, maybe a year, do you think you would be ready then?"

"Maybe," said the girl. Then she nodded. "Yes. Yes, I'm sure of it."

"Well," said Quoneel, "it wouldn't be much of a test then, would it?"

The woman was sobbing now, quiet little sobs that moved her shoulders.

"I can't kill her," the girl explained.

"Then I will," said her master. "And before her heart has stopped beating I will have killed you, also."

The girl gripped the knife. "I'd fight you."

"You'd lose. This woman will die today whatever you decide. Make the right choice and kill her quickly. If I have to do it, I'll chop her into little bits and she'll die screaming."

The girl looked at the sobbing woman, and tears came to her own eyes. "Please don't make me..."

"I am sorry, child," said Quoneel. "But this is something you must do."

The woman lunged suddenly for the door, knocking Quoneel to the side, and barrelled straight towards the girl, her face twisted in desperation and rage. She ran into the girl and stopped, and the girl stepped away, her hand empty. The woman looked down at the dagger in her belly. She sobbed again, and her legs collapsed from under her. She sat on the ground and shook her head.

"No," the woman said quietly. "No, please... not me..."

She sobbed, and took a short, rattling breath, and when she breathed out, she leaned over until her head rested on the ground. She didn't move, and she didn't take another breath.

The girl looked at her hands. No blood on them. All the woman's blood was leaking to the floor. She could hear it drip. But none on her hands. Her hands were clean. She didn't think that was right. They should be stained red. She thought about kneeling down, putting her hands in the growing pool of blood, but the idea, the very idea, was making something rise up in her mind, something dark and ugly and scared, and it made her body shake and the tears flow.

"You've done well," said Quoneel. "Your lessons for today are at an end. You are dismissed."

She ran from the room, tears blurring her vision.

The next morning Quoneel sat next to her as she ate. The girl wasn't used to people sitting next to her.

"Some of the children said they heard you crying last night," he said, his voice quiet but casual, like he was just asking her to pass the bread.

The girl said nothing.

"Is this true?" Quoneel asked. "Were you crying in your room, child?"

"You made me kill someone."

"Yes, I did. Is that why you wept?"

"I thought we only killed bad people. That's what you said. That's what you told me."

Quoneel shook his head. "I said we kill people for a reason. If you chose to understand that as only killing the wicked, then how can I be held responsible?"

"But if we kill good people, then we can't be good."

Quoneel smiled. "We have a code. We have guidelines. We kill people who deserve death. But sometimes those who deserve death are not wicked people."

"My brother would never kill an innocent person."

"You don't know your brother."

"I know him better than you," she said, anger flushing her face. "He's good and he's a hero and he helps people."

"He helps people, this is true. As do we all. That is why we're here, we knives in the shadows. To help people."

"Then why did you make me kill an innocent person?"

"To see if you would. To see if you could. You passed that test. The first time is always the hardest. It will be easier from now on."

"I'm not killing any more innocent people."

Quoneel smiled again. "You haven't killed any innocent people, child. That woman murdered her husband." A long pause. "You look surprised. You think all murderers look like murderers? You think they plot and scheme and twirl moustaches? She poisoned her husband to be rid of him and to get his money. She deserved death."

"What... what will happen to her children?"

"The mortals know how to deal with things like this. The children will be taken care of."

The girl looked down at her plate. "Why didn't you tell me?"

"Would it have made it easier to kill a murderer?"

The girl paused. "Yes."

"Then what kind of test would it have been?" Quoneel asked.

7

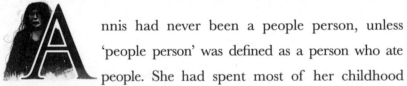nnis had never been a people person, unless 'people person' was defined as a person who ate people. She had spent most of her childhood miserable and alone while the other children in her village threw stones at her and called her names. Her teenage years had been typically awkward as a result, and then she ate everyone in her village so the opportunity for decent conversation became decidedly slimmer. When she was sixteen, the sun started to turn her to stone, so her entire adult life was spent in a variety of caves and ditches where her only source of friendship had been Scrannal, an idiot. So being in a room with other people was an

unusual and unsettling development, and one which she hadn't planned on... and then *he* walked in.

Annis felt her heart surge in her chest. Her belly squirmed like it was filled with a hundred undigested snakes. She felt blood rush to her face and hoped desperately that she wasn't turning blue. Was this it? Was this what so many of her screaming victims referred to as 'love'? Was this what they felt for the names they cried out as she devoured them?

He was tall, dark, and handsome. He had a quality about him, a mysterious, brooding quality that she found intoxicating. She could stare into his eyes and be lost forever. He didn't bother sitting. She saw that he wasn't wearing shoes. Another thing to love about this beautiful creature, this thing, this Springheeled Jack.

Black Annis was a weird one. Sabine didn't know what to make of her. She'd heard the stories, of course. Knew what Annis was capable of. But the stories she'd heard were of a wild woman with jagged teeth and jagged nails and impenetrable blue skin. The person seated across from her wasn't blue. She was squat in both frame and face, and her long, untamed hair was streaked with grey. She was somewhere over two hundred years old and Sabine reckoned she could see every one of those years etched into the lines around her mouth and eyes and on her forehead and... good God, this woman's *lines* had lines. She looked her age and then some, unlike sorcerers and certain other creatures who had a pleasing habit of retaining their youth. Like vampires.

Sabine didn't like vampires. They were too still, like statues. And the way they moved was unnatural. No living thing should be that graceful. But there he sat, the vampire, with his beautiful face marred by a single scar. He wasn't even breathing. At least, she didn't think he was. It was hard to tell.

Her eyes drifted from Dusk to Springheeled Jack, a creature who couldn't seem to stay still. When he was in his chair, the hardened nails of his long fingers beat a rapid rhythm against the tabletop, but only moments would pass before he was on his feet again, pacing up and down like he was waiting for someone to let him out of his cage. And he *stank*. His clothes, which looked like he'd robbed them off the corpse of a Victorian gentleman, were musty, and he smelled of stale body odour. His face was long and lined and his hair – when he finally took off that battered top hat – was lank and greasy. He'd only said a few words to her so far, but they were accompanied by breath so foul she thought she might gag. And he spoke in a London accent so ridiculous she thought he was having her on.

"Luv a duck," he said, "is this meetin' gonna come to bleedin' order before or after we all die of old age?"

At the head of the table, Tanith sat and smiled. Billy-Ray Sanguine stood behind her with his square jaw and his sunglasses.

"Before we begin," Tanith said, "I'd just like to tell you all how much I appreciate your help in this matter. I know you're all going to receive a reward when it's over, but I like to think that you're helping me because you see a person who needs help, and out of the goodness of your hearts you decided to pitch in."

The others looked at her, saying nothing. Undeterred, Tanith continued.

"What we have here is a mission. Missions are exciting. You should look on this whole thing as an adventure, and just have fun."

Again, everyone looked at her. Like she was nuts.

Big, bright smile. "I have a friend who'll be arriving sometime over the next year or so," said Tanith. "She's awesome, and she'll do some pretty awesome things. But there'll be a lot of people who will want to hurt my friend, and they'll use four God-Killer weapons to do that."

Sabine shifted in her seat. "Who's your friend?"

"I'm glad you asked me that," said Tanith. "Her name's Darquesse and she's lovely. You'll love her, you really will. She's so funny and nice and she's great to hang out with."

Sabine frowned. "Isn't she the one they're saying will destroy the world?"

"OK, Sabine, for a start, I don't know why you're being so negative about this. How about waiting until you've met her before you start judging her? Think you can do that? Secondly, it's not destroying the world, it's destroying some *bits* of the world. It's like a sculptor chipping away at a rock until she gets it just right. That's what Darquesse is going to do. That's all I'm going to say about it right now, but I'm glad you asked because now the question has been answered and we can move on. Any more questions?"

Annis put up her hand.

"No questions till after," said Tanith. "Where was I? Dexter Vex has assembled a group of seven sorcerers, including himself, from different Sanctuaries around the world – Frightening Jones, Aurora Jane, Wilhelm Scream, the Monster Hunters, and his old friend and Dead Men colleague Saracen Rue. I feel, in the interest of full disclosure, I should make it known at this point that I have had relationships with both Frightening and Saracen, and a little bit of a thing with Aurora. Aurora was lovely, but it didn't work out, Frightening and I gradually drifted apart and, with Saracen, I assure you it was purely physical."

"They probably don't need to know all that," Sanguine said from behind her, his face stony.

"Vex used to have another sorcerer on his team," Tanith continued. "They had a Sensitive named Jerry. Just to let you know, I did *not* have a relationship with Jerry. Let's be clear about that. He was a rubbish Sensitive, but that's not why I didn't have a relationship with him. For a start, he wasn't my type. Reason number two, I was already in a relationship with Billy-Ray here, and I was trying my best to be monogamous."

At that, Sanguine frowned. "You were *trying?*"

"Please don't interrupt, darling," Tanith said. "Back to Jerry. As I said, he was a rubbish Sensitive, and I cut his head off. If he'd been any good at looking into the future, he'd have ducked. But he didn't, so... off with his head. Anyway, what Jerry *did* do was give us a list of possible locations where three of these weapons are being kept. We have since had these confirmed. We got the fourth from Christophe Nocturnal before he tragically died when I killed him. I'll miss Christophe, I don't mind telling you. Was he boyfriend material? Probably not, but we had a moment."

"The four locations," Sanguine prompted.

"Yes," Tanith said, focusing on the task at hand. "The first weapon we're going after will be the dagger, which is in the possession of Johann Starke. I know what you're thinking – Johann Starke, Elder with the German Sanctuary, how can we possibly sneak in and steal what we're there to steal? Well, let me just reassure you – I have a plan, and I'm fairly confident it stands a chance of not failing, if we're lucky."

"I have a question," said Jack.

"Questions later."

"You keep sayin' sneak in and sneak out and stuff. My question is—"

"No questions."

"—once this Starke bloke realises he's been robbed—"

"I'm pretty sure I said no questions."

"—the owners of the other weapons are gonna heighten security, so won't that mess up our mission?"

"First of all," Tanith said, "we have a no question rule. I literally just established it, like right there. I know you were here for that because it was two minutes ago. Now, I understand that you're used to being my enemy so your natural inclination is to do the opposite of whatever I say, but you're just going to have to get over that. Agreed?"

"I'm just askin' a—"

"Jack, please. Wait till I'm finished talking."

"You *were* finished talk—"

"Please stop interrupting me. We're a team. We're a squad. We're a gang. There is no I in any of those words."

"There's an I in menagerie," said Annis.

Tanith looked at her. "What?"

"We could be a menagerie," Annis said. "Then there'd be an I. A menagerie of, you know... criminals."

"We're not a menagerie," said Tanith. "What are we even talking about any more? We can't afford to get sidetracked here, OK? A menagerie is for animals and birds. We're not birds, Annis. We're people. Birds have wings. Birds fly. Also, they're birds. But, seeing as how the question has been asked, let's answer it. If it's so important. If you simply cannot live another moment without knowing the answer. By all means, let's waste some more time on this. Sabine."

Sabine looked up. "Yes?"

"Explain."

Sabine looked at her. "Uh..."

"Your power," Sanguine said. "Tell 'em what it is."

"Oh, yeah, OK. Well, I'm a Magiphage."

Jack frowned. "A what?"

"A Leech," said Dusk.

Sabine almost glared at the vampire before she thought better of it. "Uh, yes, I... I'm what is commonly referred to as a Leech. I can temporarily drain a sorcerer's power."

"And how does that help us?" Annis asked.

"Because there's another aspect to being a Magiphage that not a lot of people know about," said Sabine. "I can transfer – again, temporarily – a portion of magic to another person or... object."

Tanith leaned forward on her elbows, that bright smile back again. "You see? I've already had forgeries made, exact copies of these weapons – or as exact as we could get based on a couple of photographs."

"So we nick each one," said Jack, "and replace it with a forgery that Sabine here has already charged up with magic? How long will they stay charged?"

"The longest I can charge something for is a little under four days – about ninety hours," said Sabine.

"Ninety hours," Tanith repeated. "That gives us plenty of time to operate before anyone realises something's not right. No one will even know the real weapons have gone missing until we've collected all four. It is, if I do say so, a flawless plan where absolutely nothing could possibly go wrong, ever."

"The other three weapons," said Dusk. "Where are they?"

"The bow is in Chicago," Tanith said, "in the hands of mortal gangsters. Should be pretty straightforward, that one. The spear is in Poland, currently in the possession of a mad old hermit living in a cave. And the sword is here in London, and that's the one we'll be leaving till last."

"Whereabouts in London?" Jack asked.

Tanith hesitated for only an eyeblink. "Deep down in the dank recesses of the heavily fortified English Sanctuary. Should be a *doddle*. Now then, boys and girls, I hope your bags are packed, because we're off to Germany. Let's get this party started!"

Tanith jumped up and pumped her fist in the air when she said that. Everyone else just looked at her. But she left the room with an excited grin on her face like she hadn't even noticed.

Dear God, thought Sabine. *She's nuts.*

8

aracen was late – as usual. This didn't surprise Dexter Vex. Back when they had been in the Dead Men together, the only times when Saracen Rue *wasn't* late was when you needed him to step in and save your life. Not a bad habit to have, all things considered, but every now and then Vex just wished his friend would be a little more organised in the day-to-day running of things.

Everyone else was here, sharing space in the Gulfstream V that was sitting on the airfield, waiting for its one remaining passenger to finally turn up. Frightening Jones sat across from Aurora Jane. Born and raised in Africa, his deep baritone contrasted with Aurora's Californian lilt as they swapped stories about mutual acquaintances and laughed quietly. Where Frightening was immense and powerful, Aurora was small and fragile, and seemed like a stiff breeze could break her in half. Looks were, of course, deceiving. Vex had seen this little brunette with the heart-shaped face in battle. It was why he'd recruited her, after all.

Why Vex had recruited Wilhelm Scream, however, very much remained a mystery, even to himself. He watched as the young man sat on his own, nervously sipping from a bottle of flavoured water, spilling some on to his shirt and looking dismayed. Tall and lanky and pale with black hair that sat on his head like a dead crow, Wilhelm was not an immediately impressive person. But, unlike some other people who were not immediately impressive when you first met them, Wilhelm didn't get any more impressive the more you got to know him. In fact, if it were possible, he got a little *less* impressive as time wore on. Which was actually impressive in itself.

Still, he had his uses. Aside from having a passing knowledge of the language of magic, Wilhelm still had a lot of contacts within the German Sanctuary, of which he used to be a junior Administrator before he was sacked for not being very good at it. So far he had successfully steered them clear of the authorities. Vex's little group may have been made up of sorcerers from around the world, but this was an entirely unofficial mission they were embarking upon.

Gracious O'Callahan looked back from the cockpit. Not the tallest gentleman Vex had ever known, Gracious made up for his lack of height with cool hair and a relentlessly sunny outlook on things.

"Where's this eejit got to?" he asked. "If we don't take off soon, someone will realise we've stolen their jet."

Aurora broke off her conversation with Frightening, and frowned. "This is stolen? We're in a stolen jet?"

"Not stolen," said Donegan Bane from the co-pilot's seat.

"Almost stolen," Gracious corrected.

"Semi-stolen," said Donegan.

"Quasi-stolen," said Gracious.

Aurora's frown did not turn upside down. "So is it stolen or not?"

Donegan and Gracious hesitated.

"Yes," they both said together.

Aurora sagged. "Why is it," she asked, "that every time I'm around you two we end up stealing something big?"

"We always return it," Donegan said, a little defensively. "Maybe not always in one piece, or necessarily to the right person, but return it we do, and so it is not stealing, it is merely borrowing."

Gracious looked at him. "It's a little bit stealing."

"Anyone who leaves a private jet just lying around *deserves* to have it stolen."

"It wasn't lying around," said Gracious. "It was locked up tight. It took us an hour to dismantle the security system and get inside."

Donegan looked at him. "You're not helping."

Donegan Bane and Gracious O'Callahan – the Monster Hunters. Adventurers, inventors, authors of *Monster Hunting for Beginners* and its sequels, *Monster Hunting for Beginners is Probably Inadvisable* and *Seriously, Dude, Stop Monster Hunting*. Vex had first met the short, powerfully built Irishman and the tall, skinny Englishman when he was tracking a vampire through Hong Kong at the beginning of the nineteenth century. They'd saved his life, he'd saved theirs and the vampire was humanely put down by driving a train over its head. They'd all been firm friends ever since. Well, except for the vampire.

Gracious looked out on to the tarmac. "Here he comes," he said. "Sauntering, as usual."

Vex turned, watched his friend climb the steps into the plane. Saracen Rue had put on a little weight since the last time he'd seen him, but otherwise he looked fit and healthy. He wasn't as tall as Vex, but he had a glint in his eyes and a smile that seemingly no woman could resist.

Vex broke into a smile of his own as they clasped hands and bumped shoulders. "You're late."

"Couldn't be helped," said Saracen, dumping his bag on one of the tables. "I had a thing with a thing. It got complicated. But it's over now and here I am, and who do we have here? Bane and O'Callahan, you roguish devils, you. Nervous-looking chap I've never seen before, how are you doing? Frightening, don't get up, my ego couldn't take it. And Aurora. My one true soul mate. My darling. Remind me, have you and I ever fallen in love?"

Aurora sighed. "No, Saracen, we haven't."

"Do you want to change that?"

"What, now?"

"It's a long plane ride."

"You don't even know where we're going."

"That's a good point," said Saracen. "Dexter, where are we going? What's the plan? Why am I here?"

"I'll tell you as soon as we're airborne," said Vex, settling into his seat and buckling up. "Captain O'Callahan?"

Gracious nodded, started flicking some switches. "Ladies and gentlemen," he said over the speakers, "welcome aboard this recently liberated Gulfstream V. If I could have your attention for just a few moments, I'd like to go over the safety features of this aircraft. It has an engine, to make us go, and wings, to keep us in the air. There are seatbelts, which won't do you an awful lot of good if we fly into the side of a mountain."

The jet began its taxiing to the runway with a sudden lurch, and Gracious chuckled.

"Sorry about that, ladies and gentlemen. I've actually never flown one of these before, but I'm sure it's just like falling off a bike."

Donegan's voice came over the speakers now. "I think you mean riding a bike."

"What did I say?"

"Falling off a bike."

"What's the difference?"

"You want me to tell you the difference between riding a bike and falling off one?"

"I just meant that once you've flown one plane you can pretty much fly them all. Oh look. Wonder what this button does?"

"Don't touch it."

"What does it do?"

"I don't know, but don't touch it."

"It must do something, though."

"Of course it does something. It wouldn't be there if it didn't do something. But since we don't know what it does, don't touch it."

Vex raised an eyebrow at Saracen as they picked up speed. Saracen laughed, opened his mouth to talk...

"I'm going to press it," said Gracious over the speakers.

"Do not do that," said Donegan.

"It might be important. It might be the fly button."

"There is no fly button."

"On these new jets, how do you know? It might be a button that stops us from blowing up, or crashing."

"Don't say crash," said Donegan, "not when we have passengers."

"They can't hear me," said Gracious. "They can only hear me if I keep this mic button here pressed. I could be calling them all the names under the sun and they wouldn't have any idea."

"Still," said Donegan.

Outside, the runway blurred past the windows and Vex's head was pressed back into his seat.

"Hey," said Gracious over the tannoy, "you think Aurora has a boyfriend?"

"Probably," said Donegan.

"I don't think she does," said Gracious. "I think she'd have mentioned it. You think she'd go out with me?"

"Probably not."

"Why not?"

"You're short."

"I'm the same height as she is."

"Yeah, but you look like a hobbit."

"She might like that."

"She might like hairy feet?"

"My feet aren't hairy. They're masculine. So you think she'd go out with me?"

"Still no."

The jet lifted off the ground, but over the roar of the engines Gracious kept talking. "Do you think she'd go out with Saracen?"

"Probably."

"Yeah." The plane climbed higher. "I would."

"You'd go out with Saracen?"

"If I was going to date a guy, yeah. Wouldn't you?"

"Don't know. I don't think he'd be my type. You know who I would date? Frightening."

"Why Frightening?"

"I just think he'd be gentle, you know?"

"Yeah. You wouldn't date Dexter?"

"I'd be afraid I might cut myself on his abs," Donegan said, and they laughed until Gracious said, "Oh, wait, *this* is the mic button," and then the speakers cut off.

Once the plane had levelled off, Vex stood up. "OK then," he said, "as you may have guessed, the time has finally come to stop talking about collecting the four God-Killers, and just go do it. I appreciate that it's pretty short notice, but the opportunity has arisen and we might not get a better one."

"What has changed?" Frightening asked.

"Up until this point we've been waiting for the exact location of the dagger," said Vex. "We knew Johann Starke had it in his possession, but didn't know exactly where. Now we do. It's on display at his house, along with a collection of other undoubtedly priceless trinkets. We have to get to it before he hides it away again. Once we have it, we go after the others."

"It won't be easy," said Aurora.

"Which is why I have you people with me – people I would trust with my life. Apart from you, Wilhelm. No offence."

Wilhelm shook his head quickly. "No, of course not. I'm just honoured to be part of the team, and I know that if you give me a chance I will prove myself worthy of—"

"Where's the psychic?" Aurora interrupted. "Or, oh, sorry, the *clairvoyant*? Last time we were all together the air was filled with his ridiculous ramblings and pretentious claptrap. What was that he said? *I feel a great darkness, like unto a cloud upon a starless night.* Swear to God I wanted to hit him so hard."

"Sadly," Vex said, "Jerry Ordain is no longer with us. He died last year."

"Oh," said Aurora. "Oh, now I actually feel mean. Natural causes?"

"Decapitation."

"So... not *too* natural, then."

"Who killed him?" asked Saracen.

"I don't know," said Vex. "I looked into it with the time I had, but couldn't find any leads."

Aurora raised an eyebrow. "Uh, no offence or anything, Dexter, but what do *you* know about solving a murder?"

"Quite a lot," Vex said. "Skulduggery Pleasant didn't wait for the war to be over to suddenly *decide* to become a detective, you know. He'd always been one, even when he was a soldier. And Saracen and I were there. We saw him in action. Solving a mystery is fairly straightforward... mostly. You look for clues. Clues come in many forms."

"Sometimes it's a footprint," said Saracen, "sometimes it's a piece of dirt. Other times it's a word, or a name, or a reference. Sometimes the reference is obvious, sometimes it's hidden."

Vex nodded. "So you take the word or the name or the reference, and if you find more than one, then you put them together, sort them into groups and you find the thing they share. Or you take the piece of dirt, and find where it came from. Or you take the footprint, and find the foot that made it."

"And that's how you solve a mystery, is it?" Aurora asked, unimpressed. "Dirt, footprints and references? That's the grand total of what you've learned from Skulduggery?"

"Yes," said Vex. "And I applied it all to Jerry Ordain's murder, and found nothing overly suspicious."

"Apart from the fact that he'd had his head chopped off."

"You know what I mean. I couldn't see how his death was linked to the four weapons. The place was ransacked. The TV was stolen. Judging by the state of the place, it was a gang of thugs. The only neat thing about it was Jerry's head. It was a blade that did it, a sword of some kind."

All eyes flickered to Frightening.

"It wasn't me," he said, annoyed. "What, just because I use a sword, suddenly I'm a suspect? OK, I didn't exactly *like* the man. I thought he was a fraud and a charlatan and not a very good psychic. But I didn't kill him. Besides, I have an alibi. Probably. When did he die?"

"Halloween."

"I have no alibi," Frightening said miserably.

Wilhelm piped up from the corner seat. "He died last year and you didn't tell us? Why didn't you tell us? We could have all been targets."

"First of all," said Vex, "his murder might not have had anything to do with this mission. From what I've heard of Jerry since his death, he had a habit of making enemies. He'd given out a string of predictions the previous year to some very powerful and very dangerous individuals, of which exactly none came true. Statistically, that is quite incredible. Secondly, last year you had nothing to do with any of this, Wilhelm. Even if there *had* been a death squad after us, you wouldn't have been touched."

"I just want it known," said Frightening, "that I did not kill Jerry Ordain."

"I didn't either," said Aurora. "Although I wanted to."

"If his murder *was* in relation to this mission," said Saracen, "then what does that mean?"

"It means someone is out there and they don't want us to get our hands on the God-Killers," said Vex. "If this is true, we'll undoubtedly come across them over the next few days."

"Oh God," Wilhelm said.

Aurora turned to him. "I'm sorry, I don't believe we've been introduced."

"My fault," said Vex. "Aurora Jane, this is Wilhelm Scream. Wilhelm, this is Aurora and everyone."

"Hi, Wilhelm," Aurora said, smiling. "I just want to check – are you going to be complaining every minute we're on the job, or are you going to man up any time over the next few hours?"

Wilhelm went a little paler, and sank so far back into his seat he looked like he was trying to pass through it.

"Wilhelm is a good guy," Vex said. "He might not have the experience the rest of us have, but what he lacks in combat skills he more than makes up for in... Anyway, welcome aboard,

Wilhelm. Our first stop is Germany. Tomorrow night we sneak in and grab the dagger."

"Why not tonight?" Frightening asked.

"Tonight Johann Starke is having a party to show off his collection. Security will be tightened and there'll be guests everywhere. Only the very foolish or the very reckless would try to steal the dagger tonight."

9

arkness cracked and light spilled, and then Tanith was stepping out from the wall into Johann Starke's house. A four-piece orchestra played in the next room. Lots of chatter, sprinkled through with light laughter. No alarms. No cries. So far so good.

"I could go straight for the dagger," Sanguine said quietly. "Why the hell not? I'm here, ain't I? Save you the trouble of the play-acting."

Tanith unzipped her jumpsuit and let it fall to the ground. She stepped out of it, slipping her feet into high heels as she rested the delicate strap of her handbag on one shoulder. Her dress was red and tight and her hair was brown and straight. She caught a glimpse of herself in a mirror and liked what she saw.

"Starke's security system would alert every Ripper in the area," she told him. "You don't want that, do you? It'll be fine. I'll mingle, I'll charm, I'll get the dagger and replace it with the forgery. You just be waiting to pick me up."

"Do you even speak German?" he asked, scooping up the jumpsuit and being careful not to let any dust near her outfit.

"I have a few words," she said.

"Any of them not swear words?"

"*Nein.* Trust me, all right? Now, do I look amazing?"

"You always look amazing. Kiss for good luck?"

"Don't want to smudge my make-up," she said, and walked to the door. She painted an easy smile on her face. The first person she saw was a man dressed completely in black with a visored helmet and two sickles strapped to his back. A Ripper. He walked by, ignoring her completely. She took a moment to calm down, nodded to an elderly couple and then at a man with dark hair and turned like she'd forgotten something. She stepped back into the room. Sanguine hadn't left yet. He frowned at her.

"What? What's wrong?"

"Nothing," she said. "Just... A man out there. I know him from somewhere."

Sanguine's face darkened. "We're calling this off."

"No, we're not. I've got a forged dagger that will only fool people for the next ninety hours. It's too late to back out now."

"Tanith, this whole plan of yours relies on one simple thing – that nobody here has ever met you. Seeing as how most of the guests are high-up German sorcerers who never venture beyond their own little compounds, that was a fair assumption to make. But if someone here knows you—"

"I might be wrong," she said quickly.

"You said you know him."

"Maybe I've seen him, but that doesn't mean he's seen me. Even if he *has* met me, he wouldn't recognise me. That's the advantage of being a blonde who always wears brown leather – when you step out as a brunette in a knock-'em-dead red dress, you're a completely different person."

Sanguine shook his head. "We should either make a strategic retreat or find a way to isolate him. We kill him, you get the dagger, we get the hell outta Dodge."

She put her hand on his arm. "No. Leave him alone. I'm not even one hundred per cent sure I recognise him."

"You may have dated him at some point."

"I'm sorry?"

"Wouldn't be surprised. You seem to have dated most everyone else."

"Now is definitely not the time for this. I'll say this once more – I don't know who he is."

"Don't worry, I'll ask him his name as he's dying."

"Billy-Ray. Be nice."

"What do you care? You no longer have a conscience. I could slaughter everyone in this place and you'd only be mad because I didn't leave any for you."

Tanith shrugged. "Just because we *can* kill doesn't mean we have to. I don't derive any pleasure from killing people."

Sanguine looked at her oddly. "You don't? Not even a little?"

"Well," Tanith said, "maybe a little." She turned. "OK. I'm trying again."

"This is stupid. What if he does know who you are? You got no back-up here."

"Would you please trust me? Go on, go. I'll be fine."

Sanguine seemed on the verge of saying something else, but Tanith walked away before he had a chance. She stepped out, smiling again. The man with the dark hair wasn't standing there any more.

Expecting a pack of Rippers to descend on her at any moment, she followed the sounds of the party and found herself in a large gallery where everyone had congregated. Starke, she knew, was something of a collector. In the past, his collection would have paled in comparison to China Sorrows', but ever since her library blew up, Starke's was possibly the most impressive in Europe.

Starke himself was a narrow man with grey-flecked hair. His beard and moustache were intricately styled – the sign of a man who spends far too much time admiring his own jawline. Well-dressed, though, Tanith had to give him that. And he had that aura of power that all people in positions of authority seemed to possess. He saw her watching him and she looked away, walked to examine the next item in his collection, adding a little sway to her hips.

A moment later he was standing beside her.

"This is a wonderful piece," she said.

"And you have an eye for quality," he responded. He held out his hand. "I don't believe we've met."

She put her hand in his and he raised it to his lips, kissed the back of it. Tanith smiled. "My name is Tabitha. Is this your house? It really is wonderful."

"Why thank you, Tabitha. Whereabouts in France are you from?"

Tanith laughed. "Toulouse," she said. "But I'm surprised you noticed. I thought I had lost my accent long ago. I suppose it just goes to show, you cannot hide where you are from."

"And why would you want to?" Johann asked. "Toulouse is a beautiful part of the world. Some of the most beautiful women are from there, you know."

"Is that so?"

"That's what I've heard."

"Mr Starke, I do believe you are flirting with me."

Now it was Johann's turn to laugh. "It is only flirting if you're flattered."

"Then it is flirting," Tanith said.

"Tell me, Tabitha, who are you here with?"

Tanith turned her head a fraction. "My friends are over there. Forgive me, Mr Starke, I have gatecrashed. They assured me you would not mind but, well... my friends are notorious liars. But even if you kick me out this very minute, this night will still have been worth it."

"I think I can forgive you, Tabitha, but only on condition that you call me Johann."

"Then we have a deal, Johann. Tell me, what does a girl have to do to get a tour of this wonderful house?"

They left the crowd and walked to the furthest wings. The corridors were darker there. They came to a large circular room with glass walls looking out at the dark lake that cut through the forest around them. In this room there were more exhibits.

"Don't the other guests get to see these?" Tanith asked, walking from one to the next.

Johann smiled. "I'm afraid not. Only very special people get to visit this room."

"I'm a very special person, am I?"

"From what I can see, yes."

She smiled. "Are these valuable, then? Worth a lot of money?"

"There comes a point where it stops being about money," Johann said. "These items are priceless for a variety of reasons."

"What about this one?" asked Tanith, moving to the central exhibit encased in glass. "This knife?"

"That is a dagger," said Johann. "And I could tell you had an eye for quality. Have you ever heard of a God-Killer?"

"Should I have?"

"Perhaps not. Eons ago, when the Ancients rose up against the Faceless Ones, they had an assortment of weapons that could hurt them."

"Oh, I know this," said Tanith. "My mother used to read me these stories. The Sceptre, wasn't it?"

"The Sceptre was the ultimate God-Killer, yes, but there were others, too. In particular a sword, a bow, a spear and a dagger."

She frowned. "Are you saying that *this* is the dagger? But Johann, those stories are fairy tales. The Faceless Ones never really existed. There weren't really terrible old gods who used to rule the world."

Johann smiled. "For people like me, who work in the Sanctuary, such fairy tales have proven to be true more often than not."

She looked back at the dagger. "It's beautiful," she said.

"Its beauty pales in comparison to you."

Tanith bit her lower lip. "Could I... could I hold it?"

Johann smiled. "I would love to allow that, but I have strict security protocols in place. There are other items in my collection that I'm not quite so paranoid about." He shrugged and laughed, and Tanith looked disappointed.

"Oh," she said. "It's just... It's proof, you know? If those fairy tales are true, then this is... this is part of history. More than that. It's part of *myth*."

He looked at her, then at the dagger. "You know what? I think tonight was meant to happen. We were destined to meet, Tabitha. And who am I to argue with destiny?"

He waved his hand in front of the case and Tanith heard a click as the glass cover popped slightly. Johann tilted it back on its hinge.

"Be careful you don't nick yourself," he said. "One cut from this will kill. And that is no myth and no fairy tale. I have seen it myself."

Her eyes adequately bright yet cautious, she reached in and took the dagger from its stand. She turned it in her hand, admiring the weight, the balance, the way the light caught the delicate blade.

She moved her body to obscure her handbag and, with her free hand, she opened it. The fake dagger wasn't as finely balanced, but it was roughly the same weight. She took hold of it. It would do. She hoped.

"Magnificent, is it not?" Johann asked.

"I'm holding history," she breathed. "This is... this is most... thrilling." She looked over at the Ripper by the door, standing with his back to them. "Does he go everywhere with you?"

Johann glanced over his shoulder, and Tanith switched the daggers.

"Not everywhere," Johann said, looking back at her, and Tanith smiled as she put the forgery into the glass case. Johann secured the lid and waved his hand, and there was another click. No alarm sounded. The forgery hadn't been detected. Tanith relaxed. "We could go somewhere more private if you like," Johann suggested.

"It's a warm night," she said. "I'd love a moonlit stroll."

"Your wish is my command." He led her to the glass door and they stepped outside. They walked to the strip of stony beach. There was a small dock set up, but no boat in its moorings. Johann talked more about his collection and Tanith said all the right things at all the right times. Then she looked into his eyes.

"What time do the guests leave?" she asked.

"Whenever I tell them to."

"It's getting late, don't you think? Some of them might have to make a long journey home."

He smiled. "I'd better thank them for coming."

"I'll stay here, if it's all the same to you."

"Please do. I'll be back in mere minutes."

Tanith secured the handbag strap around her shoulder as she watched him go, then kicked off her shoes and walked quickly to the dock. Her fingers dug into the material of her dress and she pulled it apart, the dress splitting right down the middle. She let it fall around her feet, reached the dock in the swimsuit she'd been wearing under it, and in one fluid motion she dived into the warm water. She sliced up towards the surface and swam on, barely making a sound.

The boat was waiting for her. Jack straddled the side, a fishing pole in his hand. He watched her approach.

"I was wonderin' what was scarin' the fish," he said, as Sanguine appeared beside him and helped Tanith up.

"Did you get it?" Sabine asked.

"Would I be looking so pleased with myself if I hadn't?" Tanith responded, passing her the handbag. Sabine took out the dagger and examined it.

"The fake was excellent," she said. "It looks exactly like the real thing."

"And what about Starke?" said Jack. "Did he suspect you were a master thief, or were the smile and the dress all he was seein'?"

"He didn't suspect a thing," Tanith said, using a towel to dry herself off. "But we should probably get going before he starts looking for me."

Sanguine started up the boat and they moved off, sticking close to the small islands. Tanith secured the dagger in the lockbox, then heard something in the trees as they passed. She looked up and a Ripper dropped from the overhanging branch, sent Tanith into Sanguine, their heads cracking together. Tanith stumbled, dimly aware of the Ripper shoving Sabine into the water as the boat stalled. Jack flung himself at their attacker, his nails dragging uselessly across the Ripper's coat. He got a headbutt as a reward, and a kick to the shin, and then the Ripper was wrapping an arm round his throat.

Her good mood evaporating, Tanith fought through the pain in her head and pushed herself up, swayed a little, and went straight for the Ripper. She yanked him away from Jack who went to his knees, gasping for air. The Ripper's elbow collided with the side of Tanith's face. He followed with a punch that she dodged, but her bare feet slipped on the wet surface and she went down. She crossed her arms, blocking his kick, catching the glint of the sickle blade a moment before it slashed at her.

She threw herself back, head over heels, coming up to a crouch in time to see the sickle arcing in to take her head. She was up, both hands blocking the sickle hand, her fingers wrapping round his wrist, and she was jumping, her strong legs folding beneath her as she used his wrist as a fulcrum on which her whole body spun. Her shins smashed into his jaw. He bent over backwards, all strength leaving him even as she was landing. Her feet touched down, but she slipped again and fell into Sanguine's arms.

"Don't worry," he said, "I'm here to save you."

"I'm so lucky I have you," she replied, disentangling herself from his hands. "Jack, you OK?"

Jack spat over the side of the boat. "Nearly choked the life out of me, the git. And me with so much to live for." He stood up, and looked around. "Where's Sabine?"

Sabine pulled herself out of the water behind him, and glared up as she hung there. "You spat on me."

"Oh," Jack said. "Sorry." He held out a hand. Sabine hesitated, regarding the gnarled fingers and long nails warily, and then allowed him to help her up.

"What are we going to do with him?" she asked, looking at the unconscious Ripper. "If we let him go, he'll tell Starke we stole the dagger, but if we keep him prisoner, we'll have to take him everywhere with us."

Tanith pretended to mull it over. "That's a good question, Sabine. Whatever shall we do with this most unexpected of guests? Billy-Ray, do you have any ideas?"

"I may have one," Sanguine said, taking out his straight razor and cutting the Ripper's throat.

Sabine stumbled back. "What are you doing?" she cried. "You can't just murder people! What the hell are you doing?"

"Murdering people," Sanguine answered.

Sabine took two steps and shoved Sanguine. "He was unconscious! He was unconscious and defenceless and you murdered him!"

Sanguine grinned as Sabine shoved him again.

"Sabine," Tanith said, "Sanguine did what had to be done. We can't leave witnesses. You said it yourself — we couldn't release him or take him with us."

"I'm out," Sabine said. "I didn't agree to this. I steal things and I cheat people, but I don't kill anyone."

"No one's asking you to," said Tanith gently. "And it's because we have you on the team that we can do this with as few deaths as possible. If we didn't have you, we'd be going in guns blazing, killing whoever got in our way. Sabine, you're what some people call a godsend. You're a good influence on the rest of us. We can't afford to lose you."

"Then you promise me, right here, that there won't be any more killing from now on."

Tanith's face took on a pained expression. "I can't do that, Sabine."

"Then I'm out."

"Sabine," Tanith said, "please."

"Yeah," said Jack. "Don't go. We're a good team, you and me."

Sabine frowned. "Us two? We're not a team."

"Ain't we?" asked Jack, actually sounding surprised. He looked at Tanith. "Ain't we?"

She ignored him. "Sabine, I can make you a promise, but it's not the one you want. I can promise you that we will only kill to defend ourselves. That's fair, isn't it? That's reasonable?"

Sabine pushed her wet hair back off her face. She chewed her lip. "No more killing unconscious people," she said.

Tanith nodded. "Agreed. Billy-Ray?"

Sanguine held up three fingers. "Scout's honour."

"And no killing innocent people," said Sabine.

"I agree to that in principle," said Tanith, "providing you understand that some people just have it coming."

Jack nodded. "Innocent is a murky area where killin' is concerned."

Tanith stepped forward, took Sabine's hands in hers and looked into her eyes. "Sabine, are you with us? We need you with us. I can't do this without you."

Sabine didn't answer for a while, but it didn't matter. Tanith knew she had her.

"I'm with you," Sabine said eventually, and Tanith hugged her.

"Thank you," Tanith whispered. She broke off, found a towel and handed it to Sabine. "OK, now we've got to concentrate on finding a place to dump the body. Until it's recovered, Johann will hopefully think that I eloped with his bodyguard. It should give us plenty of time to get the other three weapons."

"Which one are we going after next?" asked Sabine, sitting on the edge of the boat as it started up.

"The bow," Tanith told her. "It's in the possession of some rather unscrupulous people."

"There might be some violence," Sanguine said over his shoulder as he steered. "There might be some blood needs spilling."

"Criminal blood," Tanith said quickly. "Bad guy blood. Not innocent blood."

"And you have my solemn oath," Jack said, patting Sabine's shoulder, "that I will only kill those what are awake, and if they ain't awake, I swear to you that I'll wake 'em up and *then* kill 'em, or kill 'em as they're wakin', dependin' on the situation and what course is called for. But they will be awake, on that you have my word."

Sabine sighed.

10

"Gravity is a fickle mistress," Quoneel said. "With the right wink and the right smile, small pockets of it can be persuaded to shift to altogether new positions. Wall-Walking is not about sticking to walls or ceilings. It is simply about not falling from them."

The girl raised her foot, placed it flat on the wall in front of her. She focused on the weight of her supporting leg.

"But this is not an easy discipline to master," Quoneel continued, walking behind her. "Are you sure it's the one for you?"

"I'm sure."

"There is no need to be hasty. Did I ever tell you about Vindick Leather?"

"Who?"

"He's a sorcerer I know of," said Quoneel. "He worships the Faceless Ones, but was born too late to fight in the war. All he ever talks about, though, is the next war, when Nefarian Serpine leads the faithful to victory. Before his surge, he reasoned that the most common discipline of magic being practised was Elemental, and he decided the most damaging aspect of Elemental magic was fire. So he ensured that fire would never harm him.

"Apparently you can set him on fire from head to toe and it would do absolutely no damage. But there is a flaw. There is no discipline that does not have a weak point. The danger of focusing on one aspect to the exclusion of all others is that the weak point tends to grow. He had no idea when he set himself on this course, because from what I've heard he has never been the brightest of sorcerers."

"What is his weak point?"

"Water."

"That's it? Just water?"

"He can't be submerged in it. Apparently he has to stand whenever he takes a bath. If he is completely submerged in water even for an instant, something bad will happen."

"Like what?"

"I don't know," said Quoneel. "But something bad. The point of the story is that he made a decision early on and he is now stuck with that decision. There is nothing he can do to change it now. When you were a child, what did you dream of?"

"I wanted to be an Elemental," the girl said truthfully.

"And then?" Quoneel asked. "As your horizons broadened, and you encountered more and more branches of Adept magic?"

"An Energy-Thrower," she said. "Or a Teleporter."

"Ah," said Quoneel. "A Teleporter. What could be more useful for a knife in the shadows than the ability to appear and disappear in the blink of an eye? A dying art, some might say. But you dismissed this notion also?"

The girl nodded. "I want to walk on walls," she said.

"Why?"

She hesitated. "So I can strike from above. So I can attack without warning."

"No, these are not your reasons."

"You're distracting me from my lesson."

"Why do you want to walk on walls?"

The girl returned her foot to the floor and sighed. "I don't know."

"You must have a reason."

"Because it's useful," she said. "And it's unexpected. And in a fight, you'd have the advantage. Everyone else fights with their feet on the ground. If you can make them fight you sideways, or fight you as you hang upside down, they're never going to get comfortable."

The master nodded thoughtfully. "And your real reason for wanting to walk on walls?"

"Because no one else is doing it!" she blurted. "All the others are choosing disciplines to help them kill. So what? We're being trained to kill. We're going to kill, anyway — we don't need to do it by shooting energy from our fingertips. For an assassin to choose a discipline like that is... is..."

"Redundant," said Quoneel.

"Yes," she said.

"I agree with you completely."

"You do?"

"Of course. What's the point of being a hidden blade if you attack with a clumsy old club? Where's the subtlety? Where's the finesse? Your friends have sadly missed the point."

"They're not my friends."

"Ah, yes. They still call you Highborn, don't they?"

"I don't talk like I used to. I don't walk around all proud and bright like I used to. But they won't stop calling me that name."

"What age are you now, girl? Thirteen? It's past time you took on a name of your own."

"I'll take my name when I'm ready," the girl said. "I won't do it just to stop them teasing me."

Quoneel smiled.

"But why don't you tell them?" she asked. "If they're choosing the wrong disciplines, why don't you just make a list of the right ones and let them pick?"

"It is not our place," the master said. "We can only hope that through our teachings and our guidance, the appropriate disciplines will become obvious. Sometimes that works. Sometimes it doesn't."

"Avaunt said she's going to be an Energy-Thrower," said the girl.

Quoneel smiled again. *"Another one who has missed the point. She will make an excellent assassin, however. They all will. But none of them will rise beyond merely excellent."*

"Will I?"

"That, I cannot say. You might, provided you live long enough. We never stop learning, in truth. You study here until your Surge, then you rejoin the world outside as one of us, and you grow older and more powerful and more accomplished... And if you're lucky, you see out your life back here, speaking these same words to some other young girl or boy, hundreds of years from now." He laughed when he saw her expression. *"I assure you, it is a lot more rewarding than it sounds."*

"If you say so."

"Let us return to your lesson, then. Enough idle talk from an idle fool. Put your foot up on the wall. First you learn to stand sideways. Then you learn to stand upside down."

Quoneel was not the only master to teach her. Sometimes the girl was introduced to sorcerers whose task it was to teach her one single thing in a day. Sometimes a week. Sometimes a month. Sometimes an hour. It wasn't just magic or combat, either. There was a man who taught her forgery. A woman who taught her carpentry. She was taught about engines and astronomy and how to pick pockets. There was a woman who taught her everything about women and a woman who taught her everything about men. And then there was a man who taught her about locks.

His name was Audoen, and he was a Wall-Walker. He asked her to open a door and she tried, but it was locked. She told him so and he nodded, then pressed his hand to the lock and it clicked open.

"How did you do that?" the girl asked.

Audoen smiled. "You have undoubtedly heard the phrase 'branches of magic', yes? Picture a tree. Elemental magic is one branch. Necromancy is another. So-called Energy-Throwing is yet another. There are many, many branches on this tree. With me so far?"

"Yes," the girl said. "I'm not stupid."

He laughed. "On each of these branches there are, shall we say, twigs. Because these 'twigs' are so low-key and in most cases passive, learning one or two of them does not interfere with your chosen discipline. For Wall-Walkers, the ability to open locks and seal doorways is a twig you can either ignore, or take advantage of. Because of the work we do, having such a talent can benefit us greatly."

"Can you teach me?"

"Are you sure? It may only be a simple twig on the tree of magic, but even so it will take time to master, and you have a lot of work to do."

"Teach me," the girl said. "I can handle it."

11

etting to Germany? Simple.

Finding Johann Starke's house? Easy.

Breaking into said house? Not a problem.

Breaking into said house while remaining undetected? Surprisingly difficult.

Kneeling here on this highly polished floor with his hands up and half a dozen sickle blades aimed at his throat, Dexter Vex wasn't exactly in the mood to look back over his plan to pick out the flaws, but he knew they were there, and that was the important thing. Hubris, he figured, was a killer.

"Mr Vex," said Johann Starke, "I have to say, I am as surprised as I am disappointed. I would not have thought a man of your reputation would stoop so low as to engage in robbery."

"Johann," Vex said, giving him a smile, "there's really no need for hostilities. Isn't there somewhere we can talk?"

"We're talking right here," said Johann, "with you and your associates on your knees and very much under arrest."

They were in a large circular room with glass walls. The sun came in through the trees that bordered the lake and the glare hit Vex right in the eyes. He risked a glance at the others. They were all calm – bemused but calm – with the possible exception of Wilhelm, who seemed to be quietly hyperventilating.

Johann walked between the Rippers that surrounded them. "Did you really think it would be so easy to steal the dagger?"

Vex frowned. "How did you know we were after the dagger?"

"Your associate is not as subtle as she thinks," Johann said.

"I am *very* subtle," Aurora responded, sounding offended. Then, "Wait, what do you mean?"

"Not you," said Johann. "The pretty lady from last night."

"This pretty lady," said Vex, "she didn't give a name, did she?"

"Please, don't insult my intelligence."

"There are plenty of things I'd insult before getting to your intelligence, Johann. Your beard for one. It looks like the beards of Fu Manchu and Ming the Merciless mated, and their bizarre mutant offspring crawled on to your face and died on your chin."

Johann sighed. "A pretty brunette. French – though the accent may have been faked. You sent her here to gather information. Where exactly the dagger was, what security was in place, what safeguards I had set up…"

"That was tricky of me," Vex murmured. "And when she had all this information?"

Johann shrugged. "She vanished, along with one of my Rippers. He is dead, I expect?"

"Sorry, Johann, I wouldn't know. I have no idea who you're talking about. I didn't send her. I didn't send anyone. If we were going to rob the dagger, we wouldn't raise your suspicions by sending someone ahead of us."

"So you'd just drop in unannounced," Johann said, "like now."

Vex shrugged. "OK, you got us. Yeah, we were going to borrow the dagger."

"Borrow it?"

"Just for a little while. We were going to return it, honest we were. Just as soon as we used it to stop Darquesse."

"Ah," said Johann, "this notorious Darquesse person that has the Sensitives so nervous."

"If she's as powerful as everyone says she's going to be, we're going to need some serious weaponry to put her down. Your dagger is a powerful weapon."

"And if you needed it so badly, why not go through official

channels? Erskine Ravel and Ghastly Bespoke are on the Council of Elders in Ireland – you could have got your friends to ask for it."

"Ah, now Johann, we both know that would have been a waste of time."

"But why?" Johann asked, all innocence.

"Because your boss sits on the Supreme Council, and the Supreme Council isn't all that happy with Ireland at the moment, now is it? So any formal request for the dagger would have been ignored."

"So instead you decide to steal it?"

"Borrow it."

"Taking without asking is stealing."

"But stealing sounds so much worse than borrowing."

"It does sound bad," Johann admitted, "but I'm afraid I have no choice. I am a stickler for the rules. Once in custody, maybe we can negotiate with your Council for your release."

"That's not going to happen, Johann. Things are kind of tricky right now as far as this international intrigue goes. You don't trust the Irish Sanctuary, they don't trust you, everyone has ulterior motives for everything else... I just can't be part of that. If you arrest us, you can use us as leverage against our friends."

"And yet you have no choice," said Johann. "You're hardly going to resist, are you? You're hardly going to use violence.

Such a thing might be seen as a provocative act between Sanctuaries."

"The Irish Council didn't send us."

"I wish I could believe you. But stockpiling powerful weapons sounds exactly like something Erskine Ravel would do before hostilities boiled over into all-out war."

"Careful now, Johann. Don't make this into something it's not."

Johann looked at the others. "I am giving you all an opportunity to co-operate," he said. "Confessing now will go a long way to securing you an early release and a comfortable stay while in our cells. You have this one chance."

Frightening didn't say anything. Aurora remained unresponsive. Saracen looked bored. Only Wilhelm seemed like he was considering the offer. Vex raised an eyebrow at him.

"I don't do well in confined spaces," Wilhelm said weakly.

"You don't do well in open spaces either," Aurora reminded him.

Wilhelm shook his head. "I'm not cut out for prison. Look at me. They'd eat me alive in there. I've seen gaol cells where you have to go to the toilet in front of other people. I can't do that. I have a shy bladder and anxious bowels."

"Wilhelm," said Johann, "what happened to you, my friend? You were once one of Deutschland's brightest stars."

"You told me I was rubbish when you fired me."

"Was that you? Oh. Well still, it is disappointing to see you associating with a criminal rabble."

"Now Johann," said Saracen, "let's not resort to name-calling. Who knows where that would lead? Why, in the heat of the moment I might be forced to remind you of some things you did in your wild and crazy youth, and then where would we be? One of us would be red-faced and embarrassed, and one of us would be me."

Johann narrowed his eyes. "I know just the gaol cell for you, Mr Rue. I think you'll really like it."

"Maybe later. Right now, though, we have a job to do."

"You are going nowhere. We have you, we have your colleagues, there is nothing—"

Vex laughed, and Johann returned his attention to him.

"Something is funny?"

"Something is funny, yes," said Vex. "How many of the Dead Men were there, Johann? At any one time, how many of us were there?"

Johann took a moment before answering. "Seven," he said.

"That's right. Seven. A good number for any group of people, I've always thought. The Seven Samurai. The Magnificent Seven. Seven Dwarves."

"Seven Brides for Seven Brothers," Saracen added.

"Exactly," said Vex. "Seven of them. And seven Dead Men. So why would you think that when it came time to lead my own little group of warriors, I'd only have five?"

"Very well," said Johann, "so there are two more at large. We will find them and—"

"You don't have to find them," Frightening said. "They've found you."

Johann frowned, then noticed the little red dots that were circling his chest. He stiffened.

"Did I tell you how much I love your glass walls?" Vex asked. "Because I really, really love them."

"You would not dare give the order," said Johann.

"It's not my order to give," said Vex. "They'll take the shot if they think the mission's compromised. We're free agents, Johann, like I said. We're not sanctioned by any Sanctuary. Killing you would be no act of war – it would be the simple removal of an obstacle. So, we're going to walk out of here, because this mysterious woman has just changed everything for us. Up till now, I thought we had the luxury of time – obviously I was wrong. So you're going to let us go, Johann, and then you're going to take your dagger and hide it away in the deepest, darkest vault you can find, and when Darquesse turns up, you can hand it over to us and beg us to save you."

One of the red dots was now on the tip of Johann's nose.

"Stand down," Johann said, and the Rippers put away their sickles. Vex and the others stood up.

"Thanks awfully," said Vex. "We'd stay and chat, we really would, but apparently we're in a race, and we're already behind."

12

Pretty cold air in Chicago, and that's no mistake. London could be cold, too, could be freezing, but London didn't have buildings as tall as Chicago's.

Jack stood on the tallest he could find, his toes curled, toenails digging into the concrete to keep the winds from just blowing him off like a leaf from a tree. He pictured himself falling lightly, tossed and turned by that wind that was rushing around him, caught in its currents, ebbs and flows. He might even look graceful, falling like that. Course, he wouldn't be looking quite so graceful when he hit the ground. Not nearly so graceful as a leaf from a tree, coming to a gentle stop on the pavement – or sidewalk, as they called it here. Nope, if Jack were snatched from this rooftop and fell all that way, no matter how gracefully he was falling or not, as the case may be, he'd still end up a splatted smear of red across grey.

Wouldn't that be something, though? To go from who he was, what he was, whatever he was, to just the essence of him. At his essence, what was he? Blood and bone and cartilage and flesh. That's how he'd end up, down there, after the fall. Blood and bone and cartilage and flesh all mushed together. The bones pulverised. The flesh burst. The cartilage crushed. The blood... everywhere.

What would they say, when he was gone? Would they pick at his remains, run them through a sieve of some sort to try and figure out what manner of creature he had been? Would they mourn the extinction of a species? Was he even a species? Does one specimen make a species?

One thing he knew – no one would mourn for him, for plain old Springheeled Jack. He had no friends to tell stories about him once he was gone, no family to remember him fondly. What legacy was he leaving behind? Dead bodies? There weren't even any of those – not after he was done with them. Bloke's got to eat, after all. He'd lived hundreds of years and all he had to show for it was a list nobody would ever compile of people who went out one evening and never returned home. He was leaving voids in his wake, patches of empty space where the missing people should have been. That was it. The grand total of his many years.

Jack adjusted his top hat and launched himself from the rooftop, the bright lights of the street blurring below him into streams of red and yellow, eclipsed by a broad expanse of darkness as the next building came to a stop beneath his feet. He danced up, as high as he could go, threw himself back and flipped, arms out and legs together, falling like a crucifix. He watched himself in the windows as he fell, then curled his body beneath him, and struck out, his feet slamming into the side of the building, propelling himself across the gap to the building on the other side. Fingers digging into the concrete, he stayed there for a moment, his eyes closed, listening to the pulse of the city. He could clean up in a place like Chicago. All these tall buildings. He could run and jump and spin and dance and kill and eat and live out his life here. Safe. Secure. Anonymous. And then he could die of old age and boredom, if the world hadn't been destroyed by then.

Jack climbed to the top and sat on the edge, feet dangling.

What was the point, though? What was the point of living for all that time if you'd nothing to show for it? What was the point of living for all those years if you'd no one to share them with? Jack had never been one for self-delusion. He was aware of the facts of the matter, and the facts of the matter were that he was a hideous, hideous monster whom no one could ever love, and he was going to go through the rest of his physical existence alone. Simple as that. As simple and inescapable as that.

When he was a younger creature, he hadn't worried about such things. He was a thing-about-town, cock of the walk, the Terror of London. He'd seen it all, done most of it, and what he hadn't done he'd seen, so at least he knew what he was talking about. Back then, he hadn't thought he'd ever reach the stage where he'd be perched on the side of a building feeling sorry for himself. But that's youth. Youth's stupid.

Jack wasn't one for self-delusion, and neither was he one for denial. There was another fact of another matter, and it had been skirting the edges of his thoughts for a few days now. He hadn't wanted to put it into words because he had wanted, foolishly, to retain some sort of personal dignity. But now he didn't have a choice.

Like a schoolboy with his first crush, Jack reckoned that the little thief and confidence trickster Sabine was the best thing to ever happen in this wicked world, of which he had grown so tired and bored. Sabine was his spark. She was his light, his warmth. Her face made him smile, her smile made him giddy. When he was around her, all he wanted to do was look at her. When he wasn't around her, all he wanted to do was talk about her. It was embarrassing. Humiliating, even. He'd have been angry with her if he didn't fancy her so bloody much.

That morning, he'd found himself daydreaming. He had imagined an entire conversation where she had laughed at his jokes and hadn't flinched at his touch. Ridiculous, childish daydreams, that nevertheless made him feel so nice, and so warm, and so hopeful. Sick, the whole affair was. Sick and wrong. He was a monster, and monsters didn't have crushes on pretty girls. Thirty years old, he reckoned she was. Thirty years old, pretty as a picture. She had a pretty laugh, too. It lilted, like birdsong. It sounded especially pretty when she was laughing at something funny he had said in his daydream.

Jack stood, scowling at the city. Listen to him. Listen to the thoughts in his head. Was this any way for a grown monster to behave, especially one who had a job to do? That's what he should be focusing on, not some random little skirt he'd taken a passing fancy to.

He slipped through the window that had been left open for him. Standing next to the door, hearing the voices on the other side, he did his best to smooth down his hair. Adopting a heavy-lidded nonchalance, Jack opened the door and sauntered in.

"Jackie Earl is the man who has the bow," Tanith was saying to the others from her place at the head of the table. She glanced at him, but didn't stop talking. "He's been running organised crime in the city for almost fifteen years now, ever since he usurped the previous crime boss and his gang. Some of them were killed the old-fashioned way − bullet to the head, knife to the gut, garrotte to the throat... but some were found with arrows sticking out of them. Mr Earl may not be a sorcerer, but he knows power when he holds it in his hands."

"So what makes the bow a God-Killer?" asked Sabine. What a question. What a wonderfully incisive question that had been, and no mistake. And then she added, "Does every arrow kill?" just to prove how sharp her mind was.

"That," Tanith said, nodding, "and the fact that the arrow never misses."

"Rarely misses," Sanguine corrected.

Tanith sighed. "Fine. Rarely misses. It won't turn a corner, but it'll swerve a little in order to hit what you're aiming at. That makes the bow the most dangerous of these weapons − you don't even have to get up close."

Jack had to say something. Sabine was the first one to ask a question so he *had* to say something now. If Dusk got in there before him, or Annis, he'd lose that connection. So he took his eyes off Sabine long enough to look at Tanith, and he said, "This Earl bloke, he's obviously not shy about usin' the bow should he need to. Makes him dangerous."

"What's a little danger to people like us?" Tanith responded, smiling. "Besides, we can deal with it. He sends one of *yours* to the hospital, you send one of *his* to the morgue. *That's* the Chicago way."

Jack and the others stared at her blankly.

"Oh, come on," she said. "I can't be the only one."

Sanguine patted her shoulder. "It's OK, honeybee. I get the reference."

"We're the only two? Seriously? OK, after all this is over, we're having a movie night, and you all have to come."

Dusk's lip pulled back slightly. "I don't do movie nights."

"Fine," Tanith said, "whatever. The rest of you. Bring your popcorn."

"We should probably get back to the job," Sanguine said.

"Right," said Tanith, "yeah." She put the forged bow on the table. "Sabine, can you work your mojo?"

Sabine took the weapon and closed her eyes, and her hands started to glow as she infused the thing with magic. Jack could have watched that all night.

"Jackie Earl is hidden away in his own private compound," said Tanith, "guarded by security cameras, alarm systems and armed sentries."

And another chance arose for Jack to impress Sabine. "Mortal sentries?" he asked.

"Mostly," Tanith said. "He has a sorcerer on his staff, named Kaiven. A Necromancer."

Jack made a face at Sabine. "Never liked them," he said, but Sabine's eyes were still closed so she totally missed it.

Tanith shrugged. "Ever since the Death Bringer failed to usher in the Passage, Necromancers around the world have either retreated into the safety of their Temples or left the Order and struck out on their own. From what I've heard, Kaiven offered his services to Earl and Earl gladly took him up on it."

"So he has a Necromancer working for him," Sabine said, opening her eyes and cutting straight through to the heart of the matter as usual. She handed the bow back to Tanith, who nodded approvingly. "Anyone else we should know about?"

"Nope," said Tanith. "Not a one. Nothing."

"Honey..." said Sanguine.

"Oh, yes, thank you, nearly forgot. We've heard he *may* have a vampire, too."

Jack noticed Sabine going pale. Annis just kept chewing her hair. Only Dusk spoke.

"I cannot be a part of this."

"Let's not make any rash decisions," Tanith said.

"Vampires are forbidden from killing other vampires. It is our most sacred code."

"You don't have to kill him," Sanguine said. "You can just injure him a little. Cut off his arms and legs or something."

119

Dusk stood. "You can retrieve the bow without my involvement. Contact me when you're done." He walked out.

Jack couldn't resist. "So Dusk is missin' out on *this* job because of his principles," he said, "and he missed out on the *last* one because he's rationin' out his serum to keep his bitey side down durin' the night... So what good is our little vampire to us *at all*, may I ask?"

"He provides moral support," Tanith muttered, then she sat up straighter. "But that's fine. We can't let anything delay us. We have a little under sixty-five hours before the dagger loses its charge and Johann Starke realises he's been robbed, so we are sticking to our timetable no matter what. I'm going after the bow. Billy-Ray is going to take care of Kaiven."

"What about Sabine?" Jack asked. "I think she's proven herself to be a valuable member of this team and I think she should be treated as such."

Tanith frowned at him. "Uh, yeah, OK. Anyway, Sabine, you and Jack are going to run interference."

"Us?" said Sabine.

Jack's heart leaped. "We could do that," he said, struggling to keep the excitement from his voice.

Tanith looked to Annis then. "And Annis... Annis is going to take down the vampire. Think you can handle that, Annis?"

Annis pulled a long grey hair from her mouth. "I've never eaten a vampire before," she said.

Tanith grinned. "That's the spirit. We move out now."

"I'll make my own way there," announced Jack, and walked quickly from the room.

He slipped out of the window and leaped from building to building, trying to get rid of the smile on his face. Partnered with Sabine. It was almost too good to be true. It would have been foolish to read too much into it, but since he had a few miles to cover it was a good enough way to spend the time as any. So what did it mean? Did it mean that Tanith could see the partnership potential already? Could everyone see that? Did they look at Jack and look at Sabine and think to themselves, *Yep, those two are meant for each other*? It was like the Skeleton Detective and the Cain girl. People looked at them and said, *Now* that's *a team*. Would they say the same about Sabine and Jack? The thought sent shivers of excitement through him as he ran and jumped and dived. They'd be just like Skulduggery Pleasant and Valkyrie Cain, then, but with added kissing.

Jack laughed.

He was having so much fun up there, alone with his thoughts, that the time kind of got away from him. Chuckling at his own giddiness, he got himself back on track, and the wind picked up as he got nearer to Chicago's harbour. Jackie Earl's compound was bordered by a tall fence. The main warehouse was accessed

121

through an open courtyard with buildings on either side. Watchtowers stood in the south-east and north-west corners. By the time Jack landed on the roof, the sentries in those watchtowers had already met Tanith Low's blade.

"You're late," Sabine whispered.

Jack scanned the area, keeping his face away from her so she wouldn't see the goofy smile. She'd been worried about him.

"Tanith and Sanguine are over there," Sabine said. "Annis is that way." Jack nodded, but didn't move. This was a special moment for both of them.

Sabine checked her watch as they crouched there on the roof in the dark. Then she checked it again. Jack knew how she felt. The minutes were skipping by much too quickly.

Sabine nibbled her lip. Jack would have given anything to nibble that lip.

"Sorry?" Sabine said, looking at him.

Jack paled. "What?"

"You said something."

"No, I didn't."

"Something about a lip."

He shook his head. "It's the wind. It carries words and changes them. I didn't say lip, I said this is the *tip*. Of the iceberg. Regardin' what we came here to do. You nervous?"

"I'm fine."

She walked away a little, trying to see if Tanith and Sanguine had moved from their position. Jack followed, and smiled at her.

"I hate this waitin' around stuff," he said. "Much rather get in there, where the action is."

Sabine didn't answer. She didn't even look at him. Jack frowned. Did that mean she hadn't heard him? She probably hadn't. Not in this wind. Plus she was so preoccupied with her nerves and such that his words had probably failed to even register.

He smiled again, wider this time. "I hate this waitin' around stuff. Much rather get in there, where the action is."

Sabine frowned, and looked at him, and Jack realised she *had* heard him. "Um," she said, "right."

That familiar stench wafted towards them, of fish and dead otter.

"I hate waiting, too," said Black Annis, not looking at either of them. "I prefer being in the thick of the action."

"Didn't you use to live in a ditch?" asked Jack.

Annis mumbled something and wandered away, and Jack turned back to Sabine. "You shouldn't be nervous."

"I'm not. I'm just... I don't know why I'm doing this. Why am I helping Tanith help Darquesse? They both want to end the world. I don't want to end the world. I may have broken a few laws now and then, but I'm not... evil."

"I don't think you're evil," said Jack.

"Because I'm *not* evil," Sabine said, a little angrily. She looked upset. Jack wondered if he should hug her. "But Tanith is. You kind of forget that sometimes, but she is. She's evil."

Jack shrugged. "I wouldn't worry about it if I were you. Sometimes things happen that are good."

"That's your philosophy?"

"I... I dunno, actually. Never knew I had a philosophy. But I suppose if I did have one, yeah, that'd be it. Sometimes things happen that are good. You can have it, if you want."

"Your philosophy?"

"If yours isn't workin', you could share mine. It might relax you. You look tense. Do you want a massage?"

"I'm sorry?"

"To help you relax. I could give you a massage."

"Your nails are really long."

"Yeah, you might lose some blood, but some people say blood loss helps you relax."

"I don't think so. Thank you, though."

Jack smiled. "No problem. Do you want a foot rub?"

"No. I think I'm going to stand over there."

Jack gave her the thumbs up. "Sounds good."

She walked over to the other side of the roof, and he followed, and smiled at her. "Nice over here, ain't it?"

13

From her position on the roof, Tanith watched Kaiven issue orders to the mortal men with the guns. While keeping to the Necromancer tradition of only wearing black, everything else about Kaiven seemed golden – his blond hair, his tanned skin, his bright smile. Even the way he moved reminded her of a golden lion – proud, strong and graceful.

"Can I kill him now?" Sanguine asked from where he crouched beside her.

Tanith smiled. "What's wrong, Billy-Ray? Jealous? You think I might trade you in for a Necromancer?"

"And what would I have to be jealous about? The guy's an idiot. Look at him, preening like a damn peacock."

"All big smiles and white teeth and chiselled features..."

Sanguine looked offended. "I have chiselled features. Look. Look how chiselled they are. And my teeth are at *least* as white as his. You seriously think he's good-lookin'?"

"I do," said Tanith.

"Right," Sanguine said, and nodded. "I'm gonna kill him."

She kept her laugh soft so it wouldn't travel. "I think he's good-looking, but I think you're better looking."

"Oh," Sanguine said. "I mean, yeah. I am. I'm glad you noticed."

"But he does have better hair."

"*What?*"

"See how it falls across his forehead like that? It's long, but not too long... kind of dashing, really."

"A man's hair shouldn't be that long," Sanguine said. "Too easy to pull in a life-or-death struggle. He ain't being practical, that's what it is. He's too concerned with lookin' good, not near enough concerned with doing his damn job. That's why he's got a haircut like that. And what's he doing smiling, anyhow? The guys down there are a bunch of goons with guns, why do they need his smiles? He's eager to please, that's his problem. He wants everyone to like him. That's a sign of a weak mind."

"And you got all that from a haircut and a smile?" Tanith asked. "Your skills are impressive, Billy-Ray."

"More skills than him, I'll tell you that much. Main problem with Necromancers is that all their power is kept in a single object. You take that object away from them, they can't do nothing. With Valkyrie, it's a ring. Solomon Wreath, a cane. I don't know what this guy's special object is, but—"

"A wand," said Tanith.

Sanguine turned his head to her. "I'm sorry?"

"He keeps his magic in a wand," she said.

Sanguine took a moment, finding it hard to process the information. "He... this guy uses a wand? For real? He actually uses a wand? Like a wizard?"

"Yes."

"A sorcerer, a proper, real-life mage... one of us... waves a magic wand?"

She grinned. "You find something unusual about that?"

"I... I don't know where to start... How have they let him do that? Don't the other Necromancers have any sense of pride? What's he gonna do next, fly around on a broomstick? This ain't Harry Potter. We ain't witches and wizards. We are serious people with serious jobs and this guy—"

"Calm down, Billy-Ray," Tanith said, struggling to keep the amusement out of her voice.

"It's a stereotype," he hissed. "It's a damn stereotype and it's harmful. If this catches on, we'll have all sorts of sorcerers running around, waving wands and chanting spells. Do you know how ridiculous we'd look?"

Tanith shrugged. "I liked Harry Potter."

"This ain't about Harry Potter!"

"You liked Harry Potter as well."

"They're good books," he snapped, "but I do not agree with this wand business. All those guys down there, criminals and mobsters and gangsters, and who are they taking orders from? A wizard with a wand. How can they take him seriously? How are they going to take us seriously when we attack?"

"Hopefully they won't," said Tanith. "If they're waiting for us to wave our wands, maybe they won't shoot, and then we can kill them more easily."

Sanguine shook his head. "No. It ain't right. That guy should be ashamed of himself. I have to kill him. You know that, right? It's a point of honour. Now it... it's just a point of honour."

"If the opportunity presents itself," said Tanith, "you go right ahead and kill him."

"I will."

"Just be careful of his magic wand."

Sanguine muttered something she couldn't hear, and Tanith grinned again.

A man appeared at the window above, leaning out, talking to Kaiven. A man in his fifties, balding. Jackie Earl.

"And we have our target," Tanith murmured. "You'd better head over to Annis, give her some encouragement. Let Jack and Sabine take care of the gunmen – you focus on Kaiven. He's the only one who'll pose a problem."

"I still don't like you going after the bow alone."

"You don't think I can handle one little mobster? Please." She kissed him. "Go on now, scoot."

Looking decidedly unimpressed, Sanguine disappeared into the wall, and Tanith turned back to Earl as he closed his window.

From where she crouched on the roof, hidden in darkness like she was, Annis could peer down into the courtyard and remain completely invisible. She watched the men walk with their guns slung over their shoulders, even caught bits and pieces of their conversation. Not very interesting stuff.

She heard something behind her and fixed a smile on to her face, but it was only Sanguine.

He frowned at her. "What's wrong with your mouth?"

"Nothing," she muttered.

"Have you had a seizure?"

"It's nothing." God, he annoyed her. Why did it have to be him? Why couldn't it have been Jack? Then they could have crouched here, in the dark, waiting to kill people, and it would have been romantic. Jack wouldn't have asked whether her smile was a seizure, she knew that much.

Or maybe he would have. There was no point lying to herself. She'd seen how he looked at that little blonde thing, Sabine. At first she'd mistaken the look in his eyes for hunger. Sabine was a tasty morsel, it had to be said. She was a meal waiting to happen. Annis herself had fantasised about it. It was perfectly natural. She wasn't ashamed of her urges.

But the more she saw them together, the less sure she was that it was hunger in Jack's eyes. Or at least that *kind* of hunger. Maybe it was a hunger of a different sort. And that little piece of trash, that floozy, that Jezebel, that blonde harlot, was stringing Jack along like this was all a game. Anger burned in Annis's throat.

"Did you hear anything I just said?" Sanguine asked.

She blinked at him. "*Whu?*"

"Get your head in the game, Annis. You got a job to do."

"I know," she snapped. "I just have... things on my mind."

"Do us all a favour and focus, all right? You're the starter's pistol. You go down there, cause a distraction like only you can do. That's the signal for Jack and Sabine to start picking off the mortals and for Tanith to go after the bow."

"Where's the vampire?"

"There's a reinforced door down the other side of this courtyard – I'm assuming that's where they keep the vamp. They'll release it soon after you make yourself known, so be ready. And if you see a guy with a wand, leave him alone. He's mine."

Annis peered downwards. "How am I supposed to get down there?"

"Tanith said something about that," Sanguine told her. "Let's see, what was it? Something about the element of surprise. Oh, yeah, I remember."

He put a hand on her back and pushed, and Annis was suddenly tumbling, arms flailing as she fell, skirt up around her head. The ground came to meet her and its embrace was not soft. She bounced, rolled and lay there on her back, gasping, struggling to breathe. She looked straight up and saw Sanguine, waving down at her. Her skin started turning blue.

She heard running footsteps, getting closer, and forced herself to sit up, gritting teeth that were already lengthening in her mouth. Her fingernails were growing too. Moaning slightly, she got to her feet as half a dozen men ran up, guns in their hands. When they saw her, the men at the front pulled up short, and the ones behind ran into them. There was much cursing and shoving, but they all turned silent when her jaw popped, allowing her teeth to grow to their full size.

Black Annis stood before them, blue-skinned and wild-haired, fingernails click-clacking together and saliva dribbling down her chin.

"What the hell is that?" one of the men whispered.

Another man raised his gun. It trembled in his grip. "A monster," he said.

Annis snarled.

The men spread out from each other, forming a line. Annis looked down the barrels of all those guns. She didn't like guns. Guns hurt.

A man with a silly moustache was the first to pull the trigger. The bullet hit her in the shoulder. The others fired, then, and she staggered, bullets slamming into her torso, her legs, her head. She pitched backwards, the hard ground embracing her once again.

The gunfire stopped. The last cartridge did a little dance on the ground and went still. The smell of cordite filled the air like smog.

"Is it dead?" one of the men asked.

"I don't know," another answered. "Go over and check."

"I'm not going over," the first man said. "You go over. I'll cover you."

"You're a terrible shot."

"I'm better than you. I got three headshots there. You shot its ankle."

"I did not."

"You did," said another man. "I saw it. You're a really bad shot, Paulie. Also, your breath stinks and you wear ugly ties."

The man named Paulie didn't respond to that for a moment. Then he said, "You guys suck."

"Ah, Paulie..."

"Paulie, come on..."

"No, shut up. My wife buys me these ties, you know she does, and you know she's colour-blind and not that bright. And I'm sorry if my breath stinks or I'm not the best shot in the world. But I thought we were friends."

"We *are* friends, Paulie."

"Friends forgive each other the little things. But fine, if you want me to check on the dead monster, I'll check on the dead monster. We wouldn't want any blood to get on any of *your* ties, would we?"

Paulie came forward slowly. He stood over Annis and prodded her with his foot. Then he hunkered down.

"It's really ugly," he said. "But I think it's a she." He sounded puzzled. "And I can't see any blood."

Annis opened her eyes and Paulie jerked back, but her nails were already skewering his face. She heard the others cry out, heard them panic and reload. There was nothing they could do now, though. They were already dead, they just didn't know it yet.

She threw Paulie aside and sprang to her feet, charging them as they backed away. Every swipe brought a cry of pain and a spray of blood. One of them grabbed her and she took his arm off. Another fired point-blank into her head and caught the ricochet in his own chest. They screamed and begged and slipped on blood and Annis took the last man's head off with a single bite.

She was aware of alarms and distant shouts, and then a growling. She turned. The vampire stalked towards her. Bone-white and hairless. Big black eyes. Big teeth. A monster. Just like her.

It sprang at her and Annis went down, snarling. Claws tore at her, fangs tried ripping her throat open, but that blue skin of hers was as tough as any armour. They rolled over and over, the world doing crazy tilting somersaults all around them. Compared to her own blue hide, the vampire's alabaster skin was soft and tender, and her teeth cut through it with ease. The vampire shrieked and twisted, its claws raking across her face, almost taking out one of her eyes. The vampire was suddenly free, but she reached out, grabbed its foot, brought it down when it tried to leap away. She crawled over it, her claws leaving bloody furrows in its flesh, and its shrieks reached a new pitch of desperation and raw fear as she crawled up towards its neck.

*

Jack was happy. He whirled and twirled and killed and mobsters died all around him, and tucked back there, out of harm's way, was Sabine, watching it all. He tried not to show off, honest he did, but every now and then he'd catch himself killing with an unnecessary flourish or making a hilarious joke.

Like after a quick disembowelling: "That took guts!"

Or after he tore out a throat: "That's put an end to your singin' career!"

Or his favourite, after he'd plunged his fingers into the eyes of a gunman: "Hey, you got somethin' in your eye... oh yeah, it's me!"

Hilarious, each and every one. He didn't even have to look back to just *know* that Sabine was impressed.

Life was good for Springheeled Jack.

Sanguine rose up from the ground, snapped a goon's neck and watched Kaiven and two other gunmen turn to him. "We're just here for the bow," he said.

"You shall not pass," Kaiven thundered, raising his wand.

Sanguine lowered his head. "Please," he said, "have a little dignity. There are mortals present."

"Indeed there are," said Kaiven, "and they will open fire if you take one more step. You are not leaving here with the bow. I don't think my boss is ready to part with it just yet. Maybe if you come back in a few decades, after he's dead..."

"This is disgusting," Sanguine said. "Look at you, taking orders from a mortal. What the hell's wrong with you?"

Kaiven raised an eyebrow. "Ah, you're one of them, are you? The sorcerers who believe themselves somehow superior to the dominant species on the planet?"

"No I ain't," Sanguine replied, "but I'd still never take orders from a man who couldn't kill me in a fair fight."

"What can I say? I like my job, and the pay is good. I've been living in a Temple for the last few decades. My bedroom was a cold cell with a bunk and a privy. You really think that's any way for a grown man to live in this day and age? Now that I'm out, I have an apartment, and a jacuzzi, and a television that takes up an entire wall that is also a computer.

"I watch things now. Shows. *Gilmore Girls*. Have you seen it? I watch the reruns on my television. They talk so fast on that show. I've never known anyone to talk so fast, except on *The West Wing*. *The Wire*. I've watched that as well. Harrowing stuff, but I watched it. And *Buffy*. Now there was a show. *Firefly*, too. Cancelled before its time, that one. And all of this is provided to me by mortals. So, yes, I take my orders from a man with a limited lifespan, because I'm a part of this world now. And part of my job is making sure that people like you don't get their hands on my boss's toys. So leave here right now with all of your blood on the inside, where it's supposed to be. This is your only warning."

Sanguine didn't move for a moment, then snapped his head up. "I'm sorry, what? I dozed off for a moment there. Have we reached the part where I kill you yet?"

Kaiven sighed. "You obviously have no intention of listening to reason."

Sanguine showed him his teeth. "Reason is the last thing I'd want to listen to."

14

anith slipped through the window the moment she heard the first shot. Earl's apartment was lined with books and everything was dark wood and big, heavy and solid. An impressive apartment for a mobster. The bow rested in a cradle nailed to the wall. She crossed the carpeted floor. More gunshots now, and alarms started wailing. When she was done, she went to the door, heard footsteps. She pressed her back to the wall and the door opened. Jackie Earl hurried in, went straight for the bow.

Tanith closed the door with a soft click. She'd only taken her eyes off Earl for a moment – but when she looked back, he was standing there with an arrow nocked and aimed at her belly.

"How did you get in here?" he asked.

"I have a way with locks," she said.

He observed her without any panic showing in his eyes. "Tanith Low."

"You know me?"

"Good girl gone bad. Got one of those things, those Remnants, inside you. Rotten luck."

She shrugged. "Depends on your point of view."

"I know all about all of you. What, you think all of us mere mortals live in the dark? I've known there was magic in the world for years. Finally tracked down one of you, found out sorcerers are just like the rest of us. They like money and an easy life just as much as anyone. It kind of ruined the mystique when he started calling me sir, though. But hey, that's what money'll do to you."

"And you haven't gone public with any of this?"

"What would be the point? If people knew you existed, the whole world would change – maybe the Feds would even recruit some of you, set up a sorcerer task force to take down organised crime. No, I got no interest in outing you people. But I do like your toys."

Tanith smiled. "Then you know why I'm here."

"You can't have my bow. As you can see, I'm using it."

"Not even if I ask nicely?"

"Not even. It's just too handy. I'm not that good a shot – but all I have to do is point and release. Why would I ever give up something like that?"

"Because if you don't, I'll kill you?" Tanith suggested.

He chuckled. "And if you were closer to me with your sword drawn, I would definitely take you seriously."

"Well, if I can't threaten you, how about I bargain with you? How much will you sell it for?"

"It's not for sale."

"Of course it is."

"Not for a price you could afford."

"Mr Earl, you must realise that there is no way I'm leaving Chicago without that bow. You must know this."

He nodded. "I figured as much."

"Then you know I'll either be taking the bow after paying you, or taking the bow and wiping your blood off my boots."

"I know how dangerous you are, Miss Low. I know how dangerous your friends are. I've been listening to it all in my earpiece. You've all manner of monsters down there, don't you?"

"And I didn't even bring my vampire."

"I have no wish to go to war with you over this. So if

I have to kill you to finish this right here and now, I'll kill you."

"With all my friends outside? Really?"

He answered her smile with one of his own. "What's that on your back?"

"My sword."

"No, Miss Low, not the sword. What's in the bag?"

She hesitated, then ever so slowly reached up, pulled the bag away from her shoulder. The bow's drawstring tightened.

"Easy," she said, and unzipped the bag halfway. She showed him the bow within.

Earl laughed. "You were going to switch them? Oh, I have to say – that is clever. That is some clever thinking you've got going on, Miss Low. I'm impressed."

"Why thank you, Mr Earl. You wouldn't want to swap by any chance, would you?"

"Very nice of you to offer, but I think I'll stick with the original."

"I was afraid you'd say that."

"So what's it going to be? Do I kill you, or let you walk out of here? You'd better make up your mind fast – it's taking quite a lot of effort to not shoot you."

She kept her eyes on that arrow. It was starting to tremble. "You'd let me walk out of here? After getting so close and killing so many of your men?"

"They knew the risks," said Earl. "Yes, I'd let you go. I wouldn't advise ever setting foot in Chicago again, though."

The arrow was really trembling now. She didn't much like the idea of seeing it fly.

"I think I'll take you up on your offer," she said, stepping away from the wall and opening the door. "One piece of advice, though. There'll be another group of sorcerers stopping by, going after the same thing. You'd be doing me a big favour if you hid the bow and didn't let them get their hands on it."

"Thanks for the warning."

"No problem. One professional to another, and all that."

She went to leave.

"Miss Low?"

She looked back.

"You wouldn't want a job, would you? I have more Necromancers arriving tomorrow, but someone of your skills could go far in this racket."

She smiled. "You're sweet, and I appreciate the offer, but I have a racket of my own to get back to. You take care now, Mr Earl. And keep that bow safe."

She left, hurrying down the corridor. Around the next corner, his back to her, was a man with a gun with one hand pressed to his earpiece.

"Say again," said the man. "How many? Hello? Hello, can you hear me?"

Tanith kicked him in the side of the head. He crumpled and she took his earpiece, listened to the static and the chatter and then Earl's voice.

"There's a woman," she heard him say. "Brown leather, blonde hair. Sword on her back. Kill her. Shoot her on sight. Do not let her escape."

Tanith left the unconscious man and walked on. Mobsters. Just can't trust them.

She dispatched two more on her way down. At the bottom of the stairs was the main warehouse area. There were goons with guns in here, too, but it was no trouble to avoid them by walking along the ceiling. She flipped to the ground and approached the door, and slowed. The exit was right there, waiting for her, but it was open. Exposed. The kind of place that begged for an ambush.

She risked a peek. The body of a gunman lay crumpled. She peeked to the other side, saw another dead gunman. Smiling a little, she passed through, wary of traps, but feeling confident. Her phone buzzed.

"Cleaning up here," said Sanguine. "You about done?"

"I'm outside," she said. "Thanks for taking care of that ambush for me."

There was a pause, sounds of a scuffle, and then a yelp of pain and then Sanguine was back. "What ambush was that?"

"The two guys waiting for me to poke my head out," she said.

"As much as I like impressing you, that wasn't me. Jack, maybe?"

She frowned. "No, there's no blood."

"It wasn't Annis," said Sanguine. "She's been over this side of the compound the whole time."

"Maybe we have our very own guardian angel or something, like a patron saint of killers."

"We already got one of those."

"We do?"

"Yep. And like anyone worth anything, he's a Southern boy like me. Did you get the bow?"

She smiled. "Of course I did. I switched it the moment I got into the room, before Earl even knew I was there. Right now he thinks he has the real one and I've run off with the forgery."

"So, two down," said Sanguine.

"Two down," said Tanith.

15

"This part of your training is complete," said Quoneel. "You have done everything that has been asked of you, and here you stand, on the threshold of your new life. Beyond that door is your family. Beyond that door is the world. Are you anxious?"

"Yes," she admitted.

"And so you should be. You are free to cast off the rules and restrictions that we have placed upon you. You are no longer a child. You have had your Surge. You are nineteen years old, a woman, an adult and a sorcerer. You are your own responsibility."

"What if I don't want to go?"

Quoneel smiled. "You would choose to stay? The others still call you

Highborn, do they not? Even though Avaunt has been gone for almost a year?"

"The name has stuck," she said, "but it's lost its sting. When the others say it, it's meaningless. This is my home, Master. It's dark and cold and lonely, but... but it's my home. I don't know my family any more. I haven't spoken to my parents since I was eight. I can't remember what my brother's voice sounds like."

"Your father was a hidden blade before you. All these feelings you're experiencing, he has experienced them also. As has your brother. They will understand your reticence. I know they are looking forward to seeing you again."

"What if I don't like it out there?" she asked. "What if I can't live out there?"

"Then you will return with your tail between your legs and I will laugh at you until your pride forces you back out of that door. You have been an exemplary student, and I will miss our time together, but your lessons are far from over. As a knife in the shadows, you will continue to learn, to improve, to surpass even your own expectations. But first, you need to take a name."

"I already have," she told him. "I took it years ago."

Quoneel looked surprised. "And you kept it to yourself?"

"It was no one's business but my own, and the others were so happy calling me Highborn that I doubt they'd have changed. My name is Tanith Low."

16

aracen Rue knows things.

   That's what Dexter Vex was told all those hundreds of years ago before they first met. He couldn't remember who had introduced them – Skulduggery? Ghastly? Ravel maybe – but when he'd asked what magical discipline Saracen had chosen, he'd been assured that *Saracen Rue knows things.* That was all.

Was he a Sensitive? Did he read minds? Could he predict the future? No one knew. Did he know everything? Nope. He didn't know who this mysterious woman was, for example. He didn't know if she'd been after the dagger for selfish or noble reasons. He didn't know how far ahead of them she was. There were just some things he knew – and, in a tight spot, that was very often exactly what was needed.

Vex had asked, of course. He asked when he first met him, and he asked ten years later, and he asked ten years after that. Once every ten years, in fact, he'd ask Saracen exactly what his power was. And all Saracen would do was smile and tap his nose.

It was very, very annoying.

But for every one thing that Saracen knew, there were a hundred he didn't.

"So this Valkyrie Cain I've been hearing so much about," Saracen said as they stepped off the jet on to a small Chicago airfield. "What's she like?"

The others hurried along behind, each of them carrying a light duffel bag. Apart from Wilhelm, who was lugging a suitcase behind him.

Vex shrugged as they walked. "Everything you'd expect. Tough. Intelligent. Resourceful. She doesn't let Skulduggery get away with anything."

"More than a match?"

"From what I've seen."

"Good," said Saracen. "Good, he needs that. Needs someone to keep him on the straight and narrow."

There was a van waiting for them and they got in the front while the others piled in the back. Vex started the engine and they pulled out on to a narrow road, started driving to the city.

"How's he doing, anyway?" Saracen asked.

Vex's foot was heavy on the accelerator. "Skulduggery's Skulduggery – you know how he is."

"Yeah. Haven't talked to him in... must be five years. Last time was a few weeks after he'd killed Serpine. I just called him up to see how he was and he seemed... quiet."

"Wouldn't you be?" said Vex, glancing at him. "He'd been waiting for centuries to get his revenge on that psychopath. He finally gets it and suddenly he looks around and goes, *OK, now what?* I think Valkyrie gave him purpose again."

"So you approve?"

"Oh, I approve."

Saracen nodded. "Good enough for me. Can this thing go any faster?"

"Don't know," said Vex. "Let's find out."

They reached Jackie Earl's compound two hours later as the sun was dipping to touch the horizon. Gracious and Donegan scouted the area and Saracen went with them. By the time they got back to the van, night had fallen.

"Any sign of our mysterious brunette?" Vex asked.

"None that I could see," said Gracious, "and I was keeping an eye out. Quite a few guards, though."

"For an operation of this scale," said Donegan, "I'd kind of assumed that Earl would have a lot more hired muscle around the place."

"It's still a formidable number," Gracious added, "but I'd heard they had a vampire somewhere here."

"No sign of that," said Saracen, "but they're definitely expecting trouble."

The Monster Hunters looked at him. "We didn't see any evidence of that. How do you know?"

Saracen just tapped his nose.

"It doesn't make any difference," said Vex. "They've gone to the trouble of setting a trap, it'd be rude not to oblige."

A little before midnight, they got out of the van.

The Monster Hunters split off from them, and Vex led the way to the main entrance. Aurora used the air to yank the sentry from his rooftop. He landed painfully and Frightening choked him till he passed out. Vex was the first to step through the entrance. The courtyard was quiet. Windows above them on either side, and a door in front.

"They're getting ready to spring the trap," Saracen said softly.

"Those windows on our left? Five of them, armed with automatic weapons."

"And the windows on our right?" asked Frightening.

"Five more, but don't worry. Bane and O'Callahan have it covered. Get ready. The ambush is about to be sprung. Right... *now*."

The gunmen appeared but Frightening's eyes were already lighting up, and he sent twin streams of white energy into the nearest window. Vex heard a man cry out and then he sent an energy stream of his own into the shoulder of another, saw him spin away as his gun dropped to the courtyard. Aurora raised her hands and the air shimmered, and the three remaining gunmen opened fire. Bullets hit the wall of air, slowed to a stop and hung there. Purple energy crackled in Vex's hands. When the gunmen paused to reload, Aurora dropped the wall and Vex released the energy, taking out two of them. Frightening's eyebeams took out the third.

Saracen looked up at the windows to their right.

"How are they doing?" Frightening asked, waiting for his sight to return.

"Two down already," said Saracen. "Three down. Four. One left."

Glass smashed and a man came flying out, crunching to the ground. Gracious appeared at the window, waved down at them.

"Any idea what's next?" Vex asked, nodding at the door ahead of them.

"Five people waiting behind cover," said Saracen. "Sorcerers. Necromancers, I think. We'll need to burst through, take them by surprise. But these doors have steel bars running through them."

"Wilhelm," said Vex, "think there's a sigil you could use to sort this out?"

"Of course," Wilhelm said. He stepped forward, pulling a long piece of chalk from his pocket, followed by a compass, a protractor, a ruler and a set square.

Aurora narrowed her eyes. "Did you get those from a mathematical set?"

"Yes," said Wilhelm. "Best place to get them."

"But why do you need them?"

"Do you know how exact these symbols have to be? Everything has to be precise. If I had time on my hands like that China Sorrows, yes, I could draw sigils without taking measurements and that would be wonderful, but not all of us can be ladies of leisure with nothing to do all day but read books and learn things."

Frightening frowned. "Would you *want* to be a lady of leisure?"

"That's not what I... Please, I must give this my full attention."

They all stepped back as Wilhelm took out a battered notebook and flipped through the pages. When he found the sigil he wanted, he started sketching a rough outline on the door.

Aurora looked at Vex. "I thought you said he was practically fluent in the language of magic."

"Ah, ah, no, you're misremembering," said Vex. "I'm pretty sure I didn't say *practically*, and I certainly wouldn't have said *fluent*. And if I did, I definitely meant something else. Wilhelm has, I would say, a *passable* knowledge of the language of magic."

"And, in this context, what does passable mean? Workable? Or needs a classroom math set to copy a picture?"

"I can hear everything you're saying," Wilhelm reminded her.

"I'm aware of that," said Aurora. "Just keep drawing, there's a good boy, and try to ignore me as I mock you." She turned back to Vex. "Seriously? This clown is our sigil expert?"

Vex shrugged. "He was the only one who made himself available. Remember, I had to assemble this team as quietly as possible. I couldn't exactly advertise for the post. When Wilhelm came along, I knew he wouldn't be much good, but he's better than nothing. Not *much* better, admittedly, but he has other qualities."

"Such as?"

"He's quiet. He has manners. He doesn't speak out of turn."

"He has manners? That's it? That's what he brings to the table?"

"Like I said, it's not much, but it's something."

"It's *barely* something. It *barely* registers. The guy's inept. Look at him. Look at the way he sticks his tongue out when he draws."

"This is actually very demeaning," Wilhelm muttered.

"Hush, you," said Aurora.

"They're wondering what's taking us so long," Saracen said, eyes on the door. "They know we're here. They're getting anxious. Impatient."

Frightening took out his sword. "Let them wait," he said. "They'll know pain soon enough."

"I'm almost finished," said Wilhelm, wiping out a line with his sleeve and drawing over it.

"I never doubted you for a moment," said Vex, then looked at Aurora and spoke more softly. "I actually doubted him the whole time. He's really not very good."

Wilhelm turned. "I'm standing right in front of you. I can hear literally every sound you make."

"Wilhelm, please," said Vex, "this is a private conversation."

Wilhelm hesitated, then went back to the sigil. Vex grinned at Aurora and she grinned back.

A few seconds later, Wilhelm made a final mark with the chalk and started putting his things away. "There," he said. "Finished."

The symbol pulsed once with a grey light, and a darkening rot spread outwards through the wood. When the rot reached the steel brackets of the door, they rusted, started to flake.

"Here we go," said Vex.

Aurora snapped her palms against the air and the rotten door burst apart. Vex was the first into the dark room, followed by Frightening. A shadow whispered by his ear and he ducked and rolled, springing up and slamming into a Necromancer. They went down and there was gunfire and cries and the sounds of breaking things. Vex wrestled with the man, feeling spittle on his cheek as they rolled. He jabbed a finger into the man's eye and then started dropping elbows. When the Necromancer was unconscious, Vex got up, turned, saw Saracen snap an arm and Frightening break a jaw and saw a Necromancer with a staff running for Wilhelm.

"No, no, please!" Wilhelm shrieked, and didn't do anything to stop the staff from whacking into his skull. He crumpled and the staff twirled, gathering shadows, but Aurora pushed at the air and sent Wilhelm sliding away before the shadows turned sharp.

The Necromancer turned to her and she flicked her hand. The staff flew from his grip, but shadows grew like tightened elastic and it returned to him in an instant. He swung and Aurora ducked, lunged and grabbed him and got a foot behind his and sent him to the ground. She landed on top and hit him until he stopped moving.

"Everyone OK?" Vex asked.

"My head!" Wilhelm cried.

"Everyone else OK?"

He got a thumbs up from everyone except Wilhelm. Gracious and Donegan stepped in through the ruined door.

"We intercepted their reinforcements," said Donegan. "A few mortals with guns. No big deal."

"I almost died," said Gracious.

"You did not."

"I'm traumatised. My life flashed before my eyes."

"Your life in reruns would traumatise anyone. You're fine."

Saracen nodded to a narrow stairwell ahead of them. "That leads to Jackie Earl," he said. "He's in his office, alone. One man with a gun between us and him."

"Then let's go have a chat," said Vex. "The rest of you stay down here, keep an eye on these nice Necromancers. If they wake up, kick them until they go back to sleep again."

With Saracen behind him, Vex walked up the stairs. They got to a long corridor, and Saracen nodded to the corner up ahead.

"Hi there," said Vex loudly. "How're you doing? Having a good night? Probably not, all things considered. Yeah, we know you're there. We know you're there, armed with a... Saracen, what is it?"

"Some kind of machine pistol," said Saracen.

"See that?" said Vex. "We know you're behind the corner,

156

holding some kind of machine pistol, ready to pop out and shoot us. But you know what we are, don't you? You know we have magic. You can't kill us, my friend. Bullets only make us mad."

"If you shoot a hole through my shirt," Saracen said, "I'm going to rip your head off."

"Hear that?" said Vex. "He'll do it, too. I've seen it happen."

No answer from beyond the corner.

"We know you're nervous," said Saracen. "We know you've got a dry mouth. You're licking your lips right now. And now you've stopped. And now you're looking surprised. No, there's no one behind you. I just know things. For instance, I know there's a window opposite you. It's narrow, but I'm sure you could squeeze through if you really wanted to, and get the hell away from here. You'd have to drop your gun, of course. We can't let you leave with your gun."

"Might be the wisest option," said Vex. "And no one would think any less of you. We are scary individuals, after all. My friend Saracen here, the one who knows things, he's technically a monster. He's ten foot tall and he has extremely sharp teeth and two heads. Do you really want to face that? Really? Better run now, while you still have a—"

"He's gone," said Saracen.

They walked to the corner. On the ground beneath the open window was a machine pistol. They passed it, walked to the door at the end of the corridor. Vex waited for Saracen to give him the all-clear, then he opened the door and they walked in.

Jackie Earl sat in his swivel chair, both hands flat on the desk. To his right was a bottle of whiskey. "I don't want no trouble," he said.

Vex raised an eyebrow. "Some of your boys tried to kill us just there."

"You broke in. This is private property. They were just doing their jobs. I hope you didn't kill any of them."

"Hard to say," said Vex. "But I don't think so. Not even the Necromancers. That's quite a thing, you know, having Necromancers on your payroll."

Earl shrugged. "You got to be competitive if you want to stay in business."

While Vex wandered around the office, Saracen sat opposite Earl. "Can I ask you something, Mr Earl? It almost seems like you were waiting for us, like all this was an ambush that didn't quite go according to plan."

Earl shrugged. "My boys are always ready, what can I say?"

"But this is quite a large compound," Vex said from behind him, forcing Earl to look round. "And you only have a handful of goons with guns? I'd heard you had a small army in here, and I'd even heard rumours of a vampire. And while you do have five unconscious Necromancers downstairs, I saw no vampire tonight."

"Cutbacks," said Earl. "Had to let the vampire go."

Vex completed his tour of the office, ended up standing beside Saracen's chair. "You know why we're here."

Earl remained impressively impassive. "You're thinking of getting into the mobster business and you want some tips?"

Vex smiled. "Where's the bow, Mr Earl?"

"What bow? I don't know what you're—"

Without taking his eyes off Earl, Saracen nodded to the wall to their left. "It's behind there," he said. "Hidden compartment. Circuitry runs across the floor to the desk."

Earl paled.

"Would you mind?" Vex asked. "Just press the little secret button like a good chap."

The mobster hesitated, then reached under his desk.

"Be careful you don't accidentally knock against the gun that's hidden down there," Saracen said. "Wouldn't want it to go off by mistake."

Earl's jaw tightened, then he moved again, very slowly, and there was a loud click from the wall. Vex walked over, got his fingertips behind a large painting and pulled. It swung open, revealing the compartment. He lifted the bow clear, feeling the power that practically made the thing vibrate. There was a quiver of arrows in there, and he took that, too.

"Are these special arrows?" he asked.

"No," said Earl, speaking as if every word caused him physical pain. "Arrows are ordinary. It's the bow that gives them their power. Can I ask you to return it when you're done? It is mine, after all."

"Sorry," said Vex. "I have a feeling you'd be using it for criminal gain, and that's just unfair to all the other criminals in this fine city."

"But I paid for it. I paid a lot for it."

"Then you'd probably have been better off spending that money on something else, like a waffle iron. I love waffle irons. You can pick up a good one for, what, thirty dollars? How much did the bow cost you?"

"Half a million."

Vex hesitated. "That would have bought a *lot* of waffle irons. You probably wouldn't even need that many."

"I don't know," said Saracen. "He might really like waffles."

"That is true," said Vex. "Do you really like waffles, Mr Earl?"

Earl poured himself a drink. "You know what I hope, gentlemen? I hope you and that blonde psycho meet up and kill each other, that's what I hope."

Vex's smile faded. "And what blonde psycho would that be?"

Earl took a sip, closed his eyes to the taste and sat back in his chair. When he opened his eyes, he looked up at the ceiling. "Tanith Low. She was here last night – after the bow, same as you. She told me you'd be coming, which is why I hid it away. Didn't do a whole lot of good. Neither did those damn Necro's."

"You're sure it was Tanith Low?" Saracen asked.

Earl looked at him. "One hundred percent positive."

"Did she have anyone with her?"

"Monsters. A blue, ugly woman. A tall, ugly man who kept jumping about. She said she had a vampire too, but I didn't see it."

"What about a man in sunglasses?" Vex asked.

Earl nodded. "He was here, sure. Him and a woman. Don't know much about them, and even if I did, I wouldn't tell you. I like the thought of you two running into trouble and getting your heads cut off. Takes the sting out of losing the bow."

Vex frowned. "So she came here for this – but left without it?"

"I got the drop on her. Didn't really give her much choice."

"*You* got the drop on Tanith Low?"

"I can be pretty sneaky when I want to be. Now then, you boys gonna talk all night, or you gonna let me try to salvage what's left of my business?"

Back in the van, driving from the compound, Vex put the bow in a long case and locked it while Saracen relayed the story to the others. Frightening, behind the wheel, didn't bat an eyelid when Tanith's name was mentioned. Wilhelm, on the other hand...

"Tanith Low?" he gasped. "We're going up against Tanith Low?"

"Relax," said Aurora. "She's not that great."

"Maybe not twenty years ago when she was going out with Frightening here," said Wilhelm, "but she's changed. She's got a Remnant in her now. You know what that means? She's got no mercy. This is a woman who runs up walls and swings a sword and there is nowhere you can be safe from her. She's basically a ninja, and now that she's got no conscience? That is the definition of someone I have no intention of messing with."

"It gets worse," Saracen admitted. "It looks like Billy-Ray Sanguine is still hanging around."

"Oh great," said Wilhelm, "the hitman deluxe."

Saracen hesitated. "Plus Springheeled Jack, Black Annis, some unknown girl and... Dusk."

Wilhelm gaped. "The vampire? She has a vampire? So that's Springheeled Jack and Black Annis and a vampire against... what? Us? That's it. I quit. I'm out."

"You're not quitting," said Aurora.

"Two monsters, a vampire, a hitman and a ninja, plus whatever this mystery woman is. You know what this means? We're going to die. We are going. To die."

"Don't be so dramatic."

"You know what's dramatic? Being horribly killed by any *one* of the people I just mentioned. *That* is drama. This? This is just me quietly freaking out." Wilhelm swung around to Vex. "Please," he said, "tell me we're not continuing with this."

"We're continuing with this," Vex said, and Wilhelm moaned. "And we don't have an awful lot of time. I think we can safely assume that Tanith was the brunette Johann Starke was talking about. She tried to get the dagger, saw the amount of security and probably decided to go for an easier one first. But she didn't get it – we did. We have the bow, Johann still has the dagger and that leaves two more weapons. We have to get to them before she does."

"So where to next?" Gracious asked.

"A man named Crab," said Vex. "Tanith will leave the sword till last – that's the trickiest one. Crab has the spear – that'll be the easiest."

"If it's so easy, she probably has it already."

"If she already had it, she'd have used it to get the bow and the dagger – but using any one of the God-Killer weapons would risk alerting the owners of the others. No, she's left the spear to just before the end. A nice easy job to let her get her breath back before the big one."

"Let me guess," said Frightening, "that was our plan as well, yes?"

"Yes," Vex admitted. "This whole thing was meant to be quick and quiet. Get in, take the weapons, get out. Tanith and her little band of merry psychopaths have made a mess of that. The least we can do is return the favour."

17

anith sat in the darkness high above the stage, legs dangling from the rigging while the men sang far below her. She had never been a big opera fan. Her parents were, though, and she distinctly remembered sitting by the fire while her father played his favourite pieces on the phonograph. But that was so long ago now. That was back when some records were still cylinders, before the gramophones came along to dominate. For her, the gramophone signalled the beginning of change. Every time her brother returned home, he'd bring one of those new flat records for her collection. Duke Ellington, Cab Calloway, Louis Armstrong... He'd tell her stories about seeing these people play and even meeting some of them afterwards. She asked again and again to be allowed to accompany him on *his journeys, but he always told her no. When she was older, they said. When she'd finished her schooling.*

But those years in between were bereft of music. There had been no melodies down there in the dark, and the only rhythm was her own heartbeat, tip-tapping against her chest. Music no longer mattered.

She emerged different. She was older, of course. Bigger. Taller. Stronger. Her parents had left her there as a child, and when she had emerged blinking into the warm sunlight, she was nineteen years old. A woman. There was another World War going on and she barely knew who the sides were. She returned home and she sat with her parents by the fire while Dvořák played. On the gramophone, she noted. Conversation was stilted. They didn't know her any more and she didn't know them. It would be years before she realised that she'd need to forgive them for abandoning her, and it was only then that she could let herself love them again.

They had to leave the house soon after her return because of the air raids. Her parents travelled to Scotland. Tanith's new duties as a hidden blade took her on a different path. And she started paying attention to music again. But try as she might, she couldn't find that sense of delight she used to feel. And then the fifties came, and brought with them Nina Simone and Elvis and Chuck Berry. She did her best to ignore Pat Boone and found a spark of that old delight that only burned brighter with the advent of the sixties and the Beatles and the Stones and long-haired hippies and free love, and she was right in the middle of it all, forty years old and looking half that age. Magical and powerful and beautiful and trained to kill.

That might have been what did it. Surrounding herself with flower people and singing 'Give Peace a Chance' at Vietnam rallies might have been just the thing she needed to plant the seed in her head that maybe, just maybe, she didn't want to spend the rest of her life killing people. She already had blood on her hands. How many murderers, thieves, traitors and conspirators had she killed by the early seventies? She didn't want to know. They were scarcely innocent, but that had stopped mattering a long time ago.

Maybe it was the flower people. Maybe it was John and Yoko, spending days in that bed. Whatever it was, whatever made her decide to quit, it was accompanied by music. Not this *music, as she sat in this opera house twenty years later, unseen by all those people below her, and not the music of today, not Nirvana or Curve or Jeff Buckley, but music nonetheless. Zeppelin. Sabbath. Bowie. To someone, of course, Luciano Pavarotti was their Robert Plant. Maybe even to the man she was here to protect. She spied him over there, sitting in his private box, eyes on the Three Tenors. The box was dark and otherwise empty. She only knew two things about him – she knew where he'd be sitting tonight and she knew someone wanted him dead. She didn't even know his name.*

A shadow moved past the outline of the door behind him, and Tanith tensed. It came back, hovered there a moment before slowly moving away again.

Tanith stood, climbed the rigging to the very top and folded her body till her feet touched the ceiling. Using one hand to keep the sword on her back from slipping out of its scabbard, she hurried upside down along the curved dome to the open balcony. A woman in black stood at the door to the target's box, a sword in her hand. No one around. Tanith flipped almost soundlessly to the red carpet, but the woman in black heard her anyway and spun.

They looked at each other for a moment, and the woman in black narrowed her eyes. "Highborn?" she said.

Tanith's heart wanted to leap to her throat. She forced herself to smile, to keep her voice level. "Hello, Avaunt," she said.

Avaunt stepped away from the door. "They told me about you," she said. "You abandoned us."

God, Tanith's throat was dry. "There is no law against leaving. My brother did it."

"Another traitor," said Avaunt. "And now you've joined him in his disgrace. Little Miss Highborn. Too good for the rest of us."

Moving slowly, Tanith slid out her sword as Avaunt drew closer. "I never really understood where all this animosity came from," she said, "and now that I finally have the chance to ask, I realise I just don't care any more. You're here to kill a man. I'm here to stop you."

Avaunt laughed. "You? What can you do? Are you going to run up a wall a few times and hope to make me so dizzy that I pass out?"

"It doesn't have to go down like this. You could just walk away."

"I am a hidden blade, a knife in the shadows. I do not walk away. Why do you care who I kill? What has any of this to do with you?"

168

"It's my job now," Tanith said. "I help Sanctuaries around the world, hunting down criminals, fighting monsters, that sort of thing. I save people."

"You're an assassin, you ridiculous tart."

"Ex-assassin," said Tanith.

"And you really think you can stop me? I've always been twice the fighter you ever were, Highborn. You should scurry away before you annoy me."

"I could," Tanith conceded, "but seeing as how we both have swords, what do you say we fight to the death instead?"

Avaunt grinned. "You read my mind."

She came in with blade flashing and Tanith blocked and blocked again and stepped back and kept blocking. Avaunt's eyes burned with determination, her lip curled in hatred. She was right, of course. Avaunt had always been the best. Down there in the cold and the dark, her practice sword would smack against Tanith's fingers, her arms, her head. She had something – a raw aggressiveness, an eagerness to inflict pain that Tanith had always lacked. But it wasn't a practice sword Avaunt wielded tonight, and if Tanith were to survive, she needed to do something she'd never managed to do before – she needed to beat her.

Tanith jumped over a low swipe and turned her body sideways so her feet settled on the wall as she answered with a swipe of her own. Avaunt cursed, caught off balance. She stumbled and Tanith walked sideways, her sword clanging against Avaunt's, keeping the pressure on, forcing her back. Avaunt lunged and Tanith flipped so that she was upside down and Avaunt passed beneath her. Tanith's blade opened up her shoulder and Avaunt hissed. Energy crackled around her hands, but she needed both of them to hold the sword.

Just as Avaunt was getting the measure of her upside down, Tanith dropped to the floor and spun, opening a long slash across Avaunt's thigh. Avaunt hobbled back a few steps and Tanith pressed the advantage. Avaunt's guard was getting weaker. Her blocks were being pushed aside by Tanith's overpowering strength. It was all so easy. It was all so incredibly easy.

Their blades locked and Avaunt did something, moved somehow, and Tanith felt an impact against her hips and the world tilted and she was on the ground and her hands were free.

Where the hell was her sword?

She rolled to avoid Avaunt's blade, somersaulted back and came up in a crouch. She sprang at Avaunt and they wrestled, firing headbutts at each other. Avaunt's grip loosened and Tanith snatched the sword away and turned and an elbow cracked into her jaw.

Tanith fell straight back. She hit the carpet and lay there. A hazy image grew sharper. Avaunt, standing over her with energy crackling in her hand.

The door opened behind her and the target, a bald man with broad shoulders, stepped out. Avaunt spun, fired a bolt of energy that he twisted his body to avoid. The energy scorched the wall over his right shoulder, but he remained calm. He looked bored, even.

Avaunt grabbed her sword and leaped, swinging for his neck. The bald man closed his fingers round the blade.

Avaunt froze and Tanith stared. That sword should have cut through *his hand like it wasn't even there. Instead the blade was locked in place, like it had embedded itself in a tree trunk. And there wasn't even any blood.*

Furiously, Avaunt tried pulling the sword away, but the bald man took it from her hands and tightened his grip and the blade shattered. She rammed a fist into his side, but it was she who grunted in pain. She kicked at his knee and her foot bounced off. She kicked him between the legs and he didn't even raise an eyebrow.

Avaunt stepped away, her eyes wide. She curled her fingers and energy crackled, and she jumped at him and he reached out, grabbed her throat and squeezed. Above the singing there was a strange sound, a cross between a snap and a pop, and Avaunt fell lifeless to the carpet.

The bald man was already looking at Tanith. "Who sent her?" he asked.

Tanith struggled to her feet. "I don't know. I heard from a guy who heard a rumour. I just knew that someone with some connection to the Irish Sanctuary was going to be targeted here tonight. Do you know of anyone who'd want you dead?"

His eyes were a startling blue. "I have many enemies," he said. "It may have been one of them. It may have been my sister. What's your name?"

"Tanith," she said. "Tanith Low."

"Thank you, Tanith. You risked your life to save mine."

She picked up her sword, returned it to its scabbard. "Pardon me, but I don't think your life needed saving."

"You weren't to know that," said the bald man. "You had better leave, however, before a member of staff appears."

"Yeah," said Tanith, and turned to go.

"Do you know who she was?" asked the bald man.

She looked back. "Her name was Avaunt. We trained together."

"I see. Was she your friend?"

Tanith hesitated. "The closest thing I had to one."

18

ravelling to Poland was not a straightforward task with monsters in the group. Dusk had to be kept under close scrutiny during the night, Annis had to be kept out of the sun during the day, and Springheeled Jack had to be hidden from view at all times. When Tanith had grabbed the bow, they had sixty-four hours until the dagger lost its charge and Johann Starke spread the word about the forgeries. Loads of time, she'd figured. But now those hours had trickled away until there were only twenty-five left with two more weapons to go – and Dexter Vex had a bloody jet plane at his disposal.

Tanith could practically feel him breathing down her neck,

and she was starting to get nervous. Failure at this point could have disastrous consequences for Darquesse, and that wonderful future that Tanith had seen, of blood and death and desolation, could crumble to nothing before it even had a chance to spring into existence.

But she couldn't lose hope. The Remnant had gifted her with many things, wisdom and memories and skills beyond her experience, but she'd brought a lot to the table as well. A keen sense of style, a wicked sense of humour, a fine edge of determination, and a whole heap of optimism. She was Tanith Low, for God's sake. If anyone could pull this off, it was going to be her.

Of course, she'd probably have a runny nose when she did it. It was cold in Poland. She hadn't spent an awful lot of time there over the years, but she knew it wasn't always as cold as this. The last time she was there the sun had been shining and she'd had to resist the urge to go skinny-dipping.

She laid the bike on to its kickstand. Hanging the helmet off one of the handlebars, she wrapped her coat round herself and made her way down to the beach. No skinny-dipping today, she reckoned. The sea churned against the pebbled beach and a light rain spat down at her. She walked to the rocks and after a few minutes found the cave.

"Hello," she called. "Do you have a minute? I'd like a chat."

The sound of the wind through the cave was like a great beast yawning.

"Crab," she called. "Don't make me come in there after you."

A few moments later, a man emerged from the darkness. He looked to be in his seventies, with long grey hair and a long grey beard that hung in matted clumps. He held a long spear in his right hand. Despite the cold he was wearing only a loincloth.

"It's OK," Tanith told him, "I'll wait here until you put on some trousers."

"Why have you come?" said the old man in perfect English, seemingly unaware that his loincloth was more loin than cloth.

"For the spear," Tanith said. "Want to give it to me? I'm trying my very best not to look down. The least you can do is give me the spear."

"The spear is not for sale," said Crab.

"I wasn't planning on buying it." She took out her sword.

"I see," said Crab. "And if I do not gift you with it?"

"I'll take it from you and you won't enjoy it. Seriously, old man, take the easy way out here."

"The spear is mine."

"Now you're being childish."

"It is too powerful a weapon to let fall into the hands of one so young and impetuous. You should go home. You will find only death upon this beach. I take no pleasure in killing, though I do it so well."

"I like the way you talk," Tanith said.

"If you like my words, take them and run. Don't make me kill one as young as you."

"I'm older than I look," Tanith said, and sprang. Crab thrust his spear towards her and she batted it away with her blade, but he was already moving out of range as she landed. She stalked him as he moved away from the cave.

"I have seen a thousand years," said Crab. "I have seen empires rise and fall. I have seen the patterns in which men live, the ebb and flow of the tide of history. Each wave that breaks upon the shore thinks itself the first, but there have been many before it, and there will be many long after it has broken, and drawn back to the sea. I am an old man."

"And I have lifetimes inside me," said Tanith. "I'm the girl you see standing here, and I'm a cranky old professor, and I'm a peace-loving man, and I'm a killer and a maid and a king and a peasant. I am a dozen more. You think you're old?" Tanith let her lips turn black and her veins show. "You got *nothing* on me."

She lunged, but the spear rose to meet her. She dodged left, trying to get around it, but Crab was nimble and the spear tip whispered by her face. She stumbled back.

"Then I am sorry," Crab said. "Whoever you once were, you

are no longer. You are now a Remnant, and as such you are undeserving of my mercy. You will die here, on this beach. That is as much as I can give you."

He took a sudden step forward, and his spear came at Tanith's head so fast she let out a curse as she knocked it away. It didn't go far, however, and nearly sliced her throat open on the return swing. It darted at her like a snake – it was all she could do to keep it from drawing blood. The sand wasn't helping matters. She hated fighting on sand. Always had.

Tanith's blade slashed at the spear and she spun and jumped, but Crab sidestepped, cracked the shaft against her head. She went down, tumbled, rolling to her feet as the spear jabbed, almost catching her. She blocked, blocked again, backing up as Crab advanced, the spear flicking at her low and then high, darting at her belly and then her arm. She couldn't get close to him. The spear was too long and her sword was too short.

She tried flipping away, but her feet sank into the sand before take-off, and she ended up throwing herself awkwardly back. She scrambled up, ripping off her coat. She wrapped it round her left forearm as Crab came at her. Using the coat as a shield to deflect his attacks, she took the fight to him. Now it was his turn to back away, as her sword got closer with every step she took. His eyes were widening, she saw. She grinned.

He stumbled in the sand and she flung her left arm wide, her coat wrapping round the spear. She yanked it from his grip and the spear fell somewhere behind her. Crab scrambled back on his hands, came up in a crouch. Tanith let her coat drop as she walked towards him, twirling her sword.

"Lovely day for it," she said.

He backed up on to the wet sand, which sucked lightly at his bare feet. It was greedier with Tanith's boot, and she retreated on to firmer ground before she lost her advantage. Crab's beard twitched, and she realised he was smiling. She couldn't get to him without sacrificing her agility, and the spear was too far behind her to be sure of reaching it before he did. He was quicker than he looked, and light.

She started backing up slowly. He followed, closing the gap ever so slightly. She risked a glance behind, to check where the spear had landed, and Crab charged, bare feet padding across the sand like it was a running track. She slashed at him and he rolled beneath her blade, taking her legs from under her. She hit the ground and he scuttled on to her back, wrapping his legs round her waist as she struggled to get up. He pulled her hair, exposing her throat, wrapping an arm round. She let go of the sword and got to her feet, staggering, the old hermit clinging to her. Her feet plunged into wet sand and she fell and they rolled into the cold surf. Her hands were at his arm to loosen the choke while she tried twisting her hips to escape the grip his legs had on her. They rolled into the waves and for a moment Tanith was submerged.

She heaved, and now Crab was on his back. She pressed all her weight on to him, trying to force his head beneath the water, but she didn't have time to mess around. Another few seconds of this choke and she'd lose consciousness.

She dug her nails into his arm and dragged downwards. Crab repositioned his arm and the choke came back on, stronger than before, but Tanith had snatched a breath in that instant and felt her head clear. Crab's legs were still wrapped round her, his ankles crossed. She brought her own ankle up to rest against his and increased the pressure. She heard him hiss with pain. Another wave came in, stinging her eyes, and she felt the grip round her waist loosen.

She spun in place, her hands closing round Crab's throat while she sucked in a lungful of air. Fear and desperation gave the old man strength, and he bucked and kicked beneath her. She tried to straddle him, but he brought in his left leg, planted his foot on her hip, tried to shove her back. She ignored the effort. She pressed him down, beneath the water. Her hands were a vice, ever-tightening. Gradually, his struggles lessened. And then stopped altogether.

When he was dead, Tanith walked out of the sea on to the beach. Dripping wet and freezing, she picked up her sword and her coat, and then the spear. She took out her phone and dialled.

"Got it?" Sanguine asked.

"Three down," she said, shivering. "He put up more of a fight than I was expecting. Tough old guy. Could've done with some trousers."

"I ain't even gonna ask."

"What about Vex? Any sign?"

"Minutes away. The welcoming committee is in place, don't you fret. We'll meet you back at the boat."

She hung up, and took the trail off the beach to where the grasses pushed from the sand, up to the ridge where she'd left the bike. Here, a car was parked that hadn't been there before, and two people sat in it, a man and a woman. Both with their throats cut. Tanith peered through the closed window, saw the rifle lying on the back seat. Her guardian angel had struck again.

Glancing around her, she hurried to the bike and got the hell out of there.

19

Vex looked out of the window at the fields and trees of rural Poland as they whipped by, and saw the landing strip ahead. It was a small airfield with a few shacks and a tower, bridged by a fence. They came in gently, and were mere metres off the ground when Saracen sat bolt upright.

"Rocket!" he shouted.

An instant later, a flash from outside caught Vex's eye, but Aurora was already moving. She snapped her hands and the window beside her flew apart. Air rushed in as she reached out, and it was all she could do to deflect the rocket into the ground. The explosion shunted the plane sideways. It hit the landing strip and spun. Vex cracked his head and bags fell and a terrible screeching rose from beneath. The plane came to a sudden stop. Vex was out of his seat before he even knew what he was doing. He staggered for the door, Aurora right behind him, throwing it open and jumping to the tarmac.

Across the airfield, a figure in black sunglasses reloaded a rocket launcher. Vex's insides went cold as he watched Billy-Ray Sanguine bring it to his shoulder and fire.

Aurora brought her hands in, catching the rocket in a tunnel of air, veering it away just before it struck the plane. The rocket did a loop, returning to sender, but Sanguine was already sinking into the ground.

The rocket struck where Sanguine had just been crouched, the explosion almost masking the sound of a high-powered rifle. Aurora grunted, spun sideways, falling to one knee. Another shot, from the tower, barely missed her. Vex filled his hand with energy and returned fire, but his aim was off. A bullet whined past his cheek like an angry insect. Up there, the sniper had all the advantages. Vex grabbed Aurora, dragged her back to the plane. Frightening was there to haul her in. Another bullet found Vex's leg, but he managed to throw himself sideways and Frightening did the rest.

The gunman opened fire on the cockpit, and Gracious and Donegan dived back, falling on to Vex and jarring his injured leg.

"*What are they doing?*" Wilhelm was screeching. "*What are they doing?*"

"Away from the door!" Saracen shouted. "Move back!"

Someone, probably Frightening, grabbed Vex and pulled him backwards. Gracious had Aurora, who was bleeding from a wound in her side. Vex glanced at the door in time to see Sanguine rise up from the ground outside and throw something in before disappearing again.

"Grenade!" Vex roared.

But Aurora was already on it. Both hands splayed and a cocoon of air shimmered around the grenade and the explosion rocked the plane. Vex fell on top of Frightening and someone fell on top of him, but his eyes were closed and he couldn't hear and he didn't know what the hell was going on. He smelled smoke.

He opened his eyes, waited until he could focus again. His ears were ringing. His body was dull. He could feel the tangle of limbs in which he was caught – someone's knee was pressing into his back, an elbow was digging into his jaw – but they didn't hurt. He couldn't even feel the bullet in his leg.

He saw movement, and it took a moment to recognise Donegan, crawling for the cargo door at the rear of the cabin. He pushed it open, looked back to shout to the others, and a hand reached down and grabbed him. Before Vex could even sit up, Donegan was pulled from sight.

Sounds from the roof of the plane. A struggle. A cry. Someone beside him cursing. Saracen, hunting around for something. A gun. He found it, pointed it at the ceiling, waited a moment and then fired once, twice. A crash from above. Someone fell past the window next to Vex. Springheeled Jack.

The sniper was still firing. Saracen moved to the door and fired back, but the bullets were getting dangerously close. Vex got up, stepped over Wilhelm who was still screeching, and knelt by Aurora.

"I need to get up to that control tower."

She grunted, held out an arm. He pulled her to her feet and they moved to the cargo door. He jumped out first, made sure the area was clear, and helped her down. They moved up along the body of the plane, waited until the sniper had to reload, and then stepped out. Aurora waved her hand and the wind caught Vex, swept him into the air. It was an odd feeling, and not one he relished, but Aurora's aim was perfect, and Vex tumbled for the broken window.

The vampire Dusk saw Vex coming, abandoned the reload and flipped the rifle, swinging it like a bat as Vex dropped into the tower. The rifle stock caught him across the side and the breath rushed out of him as he sprawled to the floor. Dusk hit him again, and again. Not the most effective of entries, he had to admit, but at least he was in.

Vex rolled sideways and came up in a crouch, doing his best to ignore the pain in his side and the pain in his leg and his burning lungs. Dusk was fast, even for a vampire, and he was a graceful and skilled fighter.

Dusk came swinging and Vex crashed into him. The rifle fell and Vex's fist jolted against the vampire's cheekbone. It was a satisfying connection, made Dusk drop back, and still Vex came forward, bullying Dusk backwards all the way to the corner. Dusk tried to slip out, the sneaky little vampire that he was, but Vex's left hand snaked round his head, pulling him into a clinch, while his right went to work on the face and body. In an open space, Dusk would have had the advantage, using his agility to spin and whirl and run rings round Vex. But here, trapped in the corner, this was just another street fight. And if there was one thing Vex knew, it was street fights.

He pulled Dusk's face down into a knee, then caught him with that same knee in the chest as he tried to stand back up. Dusk's legs gave out and his defence dropped, and Vex sent the punches raining down.

There was movement behind him and a hand clutched his shoulder and he went suddenly cold and gasped, stepped back, feeling like his life was being dragged out of him. He turned, saw a girl with short blonde hair and a frightened face and he pushed, shoved her away from him, and the moment the contact was broken he could breathe again. But his magic was gone.

Dusk got up, still shaky, bared his teeth and Vex slugged him across the jaw. It wasn't the first time a Leech had drained his power and it wouldn't be the last. His magic would return. In the meantime, he still had his fists.

He almost didn't notice the wall starting to crack, but at the last moment he threw himself backwards, and Sanguine's straight razor missed his throat by a hair's breadth.

"Billy-Ray," said Vex, giving him a tight smile, "it's been a while."

Sanguine brushed the dust from his suit jacket, regarding him through those sunglasses of his. Behind him, Dusk got to his feet slowly and the blonde girl, the Leech, joined them. Vex could tell, just by the expression on her face, that she wasn't a fighter. The poor thing looked terrified.

"Hasn't been long enough," Sanguine said. "Last time I saw you, you were breaking my arm."

"You *had* just tried to kill me."

"I was pretty sure I *had* killed you."

Vex pulled down his collar, showing him the old scar across the right side of his throat. "Almost," he said. "To be honest, it wasn't your best work. You seemed distracted that day."

Sanguine shrugged. "I ain't gonna lie, I had things going on.

But that's no excuse. I was hired to kill you, I should've killed you, that's just the way it is. Leaving you alive was just... well, it was unprofessional, and I apologise about that. Seen in that context, you had every right to break my arm."

"Think nothing of it," said Vex, watching the way Dusk was eyeing him.

"We can kill him now," the vampire said. "Sabine drained his magic."

Sanguine shook his head. "Afraid not. We've done what we came here to do."

Dusk's lip curled. "We came here to kill them."

"We came here to slow them down," Sanguine corrected. "If we killed any as a result, that'd be a bonus. Hey, you really want to get into a fist fight with Dexter Vex, be my guest. But Tanith already has the spear and we're about to leave for London, and they're in no fit state to come after us. Are you, Dexter?"

"I suppose we aren't," Vex replied. "But if you think you're going to get your hands on the sword, you can forget it. All it'll take is one phone call and the English Sanctuary will shut up so tight you'll never get inside."

"Do you honestly think we hadn't thought of that?" Sanguine asked, smiling. "Tanith has contingency plan after contingency plan. We'll get that sword, don't you fret."

"And the dagger?" Vex asked. "Do you really think you're

going to get another shot at that? What about the bow? We've got that safely hidden away. Tanith can have all the contingency plans in the world, but the fact of the matter is she wanted four weapons, and the only one she's got is the spear."

Sanguine's smile widened, but he didn't answer. He just shrugged, put one hand on Dusk's shoulder and another on Sabine's, then stepped back into the crumbling wall with them and disappeared.

Vex frowned. He crossed to the broken window, looked out at the smoking plane. Gracious and Frightening were seeing to Aurora's injury while Saracen and Donegan kept watch. Wilhelm poked his head out of the plane, clearly terrified. Saracen looked up, gave him a shrug. The enemy had retreated. Vex looked back at the cracked wall, his concern deepening. Something was wrong.

He limped down the steps on to the tarmac. Donegan frowned at him. "You've been shot."

"I know," said Vex. "I'm trying to be brave, but I think I might start crying. How's Aurora?"

"Aurora's fine," said Aurora through gritted teeth. "He only shot me with a little bullet. If I'm not going to cry, you can't either."

"Everyone else OK? Donegan?"

"I'm good."

"Are they gone?" Wilhelm asked.

"Yeah," said Vex. "Come on down here and put pressure on Aurora's wound."

The fear on Wilhelm's face was replaced with uneasiness. "I don't do well with blood."

"Get down here, Wilhelm."

Looking like he might throw up at the idea of it, Wilhelm came down the steps.

Saracen reloaded his gun, and stepped up beside Vex.

"Sanguine's still around," he whispered. "He's underground, listening."

"You sure?"

"Positive."

Vex nodded. "I think I know why." He turned to the others. "Tanith has the spear. We're in no fit state to take her on, not after an ambush like that."

Aurora hissed and Gracious apologised. "How'd they know?" she asked, speaking quickly to distract herself from the pain. "How'd they know where and when we'd be landing?"

"That's something I'm wondering too," said Vex. "One obvious answer is that they've got a Sensitive on their side. Other obvious answer is that we've got a traitor on ours."

Immediately, all eyes swivelled to Wilhelm, who gurgled something unintelligible.

"What did you mean in the plane?" Saracen asked. "When

you were shouting, '*What are they doing?*' Almost sounded like you couldn't believe they'd attack us while you were with us. Like that wasn't part of the plan."

"Uh," said Wilhelm. "No. What? What are you talking about? I was right there. We're all in this together. Brothers in arms. And sister. Brothers and sister in arms. United we stand, yes? I didn't tell anyone. I'm not a traitor. I swear. I hate traitors. I hate them so much. They make me so mad."

"Sanguine's moving," Saracen whispered.

"Wilhelm," said Vex. "Step over here a minute, would you?"

Wilhelm licked his lips. "Actually... actually, I don't think I want to do that." He took a step back.

"I'm not going to hurt you," said Vex.

"You look like you're going to hurt me. You all do. I thought we were friends. I thought we were a team, like the Musketeers, or the Avengers."

"We are a team, Wilhelm. And now we just want to have a team hug."

Wilhelm's eyes widened, and he started shouting. "They know! They know I'm a double agent! Help me! Request extraction! Please help—"

Sanguine's hand burst up, grabbed his ankle and yanked him into the ground before anyone could reach him. He screamed all the way down.

"They're gone," said Saracen. "Moving fast, heading east. Wilhelm's still screaming."

"Let them go," Vex said, his leg giving out. Saracen grabbed him, lowered him to the ground. "Hopefully, Wilhelm will be as much of a hindrance to them as he was to us. But we may have another problem. Gracious, could you bring me the bow?"

Gracious disappeared into the plane, emerged a few moments later with the long case. He opened it, handed Vex the weapon. Vex took an arrow, nocked it, pulled back the string.

"Careful with that," said Frightening.

Vex scanned the sky until he saw a bird, high above. He aimed, drew the string tighter and released. The arrow flew, then started to dip, and hit the ground somewhere behind the chain-link fence.

"I thought the bow never missed," said Aurora.

"The real bow doesn't," Vex said. "This isn't the real bow." He threw it to one side. "Johann's dagger, the real one... I'm pretty sure Tanith has that as well. She's in the lead here, and now she has the spear. The score is three nil to them."

The others stared at him, but not one single shoulder sagged.

"OK," said Donegan, "so we know they're going after the sword, which means we know where they'll be. And assuming Gracious and I can make the repairs to the plane in time, we won't be lagging too far behind. So we'll finally be on equal footing."

191

"Or we could just phone the English Sanctuary and tell them to prepare," said Frightening.

"Would they even listen to us?" asked Saracen. "Aurora, you're American. They might listen to you."

"And then they'll do what?" she asked. "Double security? You think that'll be enough? They've got other things to worry about."

"I don't think we should tell them," said Vex. "Tanith Low may be a Londoner, but she's spent the last few years working pretty exclusively with the Irish Sanctuary. Any action she takes against them, they'll just blame it on Ravel and Skulduggery, and they'll have their excuse to go to war."

"So what do you suggest?"

Vex shrugged. "We break into the Sanctuary and steal the sword before Tanith does, and get out before anyone is any the wiser."

Saracen laughed. "That's a ridiculously stupid idea."

"I know."

"If they discover us, they'll *definitely* go to war."

"There is that."

"And do you even have any idea *how* we'd break in?"

"Not yet."

"We could wear disguises," said Frightening.

Aurora nodded quickly. "Like a false beard. I've always wanted to wear a false beard."

Vex frowned. "But you're a woman."

"Exactly. They'd never suspect it was me."

With the help of Saracen, Vex stood. "Then it's decided. We see what we can do about this damaged aeroplane and these pesky bullet holes, then we break into the English Sanctuary, steal the sword, beat up Billy-Ray Sanguine and nobody goes to war."

20

Wilhelm Scream was not exactly a game-changer, of this Tanith was aware, and having him finally join up as the seventh member of her little team did little to inspire confidence in the others.

"Him?" said Jack, glaring at Wilhelm from where he perched on a sealed pallet. Jack had been in a bad mood ever since one of Vex's lot had shot him in the foot. "This is your secret weapon? This is your ace in the hole? He looks like he's about to cry."

Wilhelm did, actually, look like he was about to cry, but that may have had something to do with the fact that they were in a freezing cold cargo plane that apparently needed extraordinary amounts of turbulence to stay in the air. Tanith prayed that he'd hold it together for just another few minutes. At the very least, she prayed that he wouldn't throw up.

"Wilhelm is the reason we have got as far as we have," she said. "He's kept us informed as to Dexter Vex's strategy, his timetable, his roster... Wilhelm has done some incredible work for us, and I think we should thank him and admire his bravery."

She clapped, but nobody else joined in. Wilhelm said something that was lost in the roar of the plane's engines.

"Sorry, Wilhelm? What was that?"

"I was almost killed," he said again, louder this time. "The plan was you wait for us to disembark and then shoot at everyone *but* me."

"That *was* the plan," Sanguine agreed, "but then I found the rocket launcher. Wilhelm, how many times in civilian life do you get the opportunity to fire a rocket launcher at a plane? Three? Four? I had to take that opportunity, Wilhelm. Had to."

"You nearly killed me."

"And that was very inconsiderate of Billy-Ray," said Tanith, shooting Sanguine a look, "but I hope you realise his actions do not reflect the opinions of the rest of the group. We're all very happy you're here."

"I'm not," said Jack.

"I'm not, either," Annis said quickly.

"But Sabine is happy," Tanith said before anyone else could speak, "and so is Dusk. Aren't you, Dusk?"

Dusk didn't bother answering. Probably for the best.

"So," Tanith said brightly, "the final part of the mission. Three down, one to go, and here we are, heading back to merry old England. Are we excited? I certainly am, I don't mind telling you. Sabine, how long do we have until the charge on the dagger runs out?"

"Eighteen hours," Sabine answered.

That wasn't good news. That meant it would be gone before they had a chance to rob the sword. Still, no sense in worrying everyone.

"Perfect!" Tanith said brightly.

"How are we going to do it?" Sabine asked. "Breaking into the Sanctuary is suicide."

"I have a plan, don't you worry."

"We could use the weapons," said Jack. "No one would stand a chance against us then."

Tanith shook her head. "No, sorry, not using the God-Killers. What if something goes wrong? What if we're beaten? Then all the weapons will be in the hands of Grand Mage Ode. Nope, we're going in armed only with our magic, our wits, and a few swords and guns and knives."

"What about me?" Dusk asked quietly.

Tanith hesitated. "We're going to need you at your feral best, I'm afraid, so that means no serum for you."

"You'd better know what you're doing," he said. "In my vampire form I make no distinction between ally and enemy."

"And that's why we love you."

"How are we going to get inside?" Wilhelm asked. His eyes were wet and he looked queasy. He annoyed her already. "Are we going to just walk in the front door? I told you this months ago – every major Sanctuary around the world now has integrity alerts, primarily because of Mr Sanguine and his tunnelling. If he tries to pass through a wall or floor, the vibration will set off a massive security operation."

"I'm famous," Sanguine grinned.

"Billy-Ray isn't going to be tunnelling anywhere," said Tanith. "Not right away, at least. I've taken all this into account, don't you worry. He'll play his part, and the rest of you will play yours."

"You gonna split us into teams?" asked Jack. "That's a good idea, teams. I reckon I should stick with Sabine. We got good chemistry. Practically know what each other is thinkin' by now, don't we?"

Sabine looked alarmed. "I'm sorry?"

"Actually, Jack," said Tanith, "you're going to be teaming up with Billy-Ray. You're injured, so you're going to provide a distraction to get the sentries away from their posts, and that'll allow the rest of us time to sneak in through a hidden entrance."

Jack chewed a chapped lip with his yellow teeth. "I don't know. I don't think you should split up a partnership that works so well."

"Are you still talking about us?" Sabine asked.

"And my injury ain't that bad," said Jack. "OK, so I'm missin' a few toes. So what? The little gangrenous one was about to fall off anyway. I can still get the job done. Let me prove it."

Tanith sighed. "OK, fine, I'll give you a chance. When we get to London, I'll be taking a trip over the rooftops. If you can keep up, we'll talk."

"All right, then," Jack said, leaning back and winking at Sabine. It may have been Tanith's imagination, but now Sabine was looking a little airsick.

They got back to London by late evening, and Tanith and Jack took off. He lagged behind as she dashed from rooftop to rooftop. There were a few instances where she thought he'd failed to make a jump, but he always managed to clamber up. By the time they reached their destination, Jack's bandaged foot was bleeding quite badly.

"You're on distraction duty," Tanith told him as he limped up to her.

"Oh, come on!" he whined. "Because of this? It's a graze! It's a scratch!"

"You can barely stand up," she said, taking the bag from her back and removing the blueprints. The wind up there snapped at the paper.

"I'm as good as I ever was," Jack said. "Look." He went to do a backflip and landed on his face.

"Yeah," murmured Tanith, "you're in tip-top shape. Keep an eye out."

He got up, rubbed his nose while she examined the plans.

"So..." he said, and trailed off.

Tanith ignored him. He cleared his throat, but she kept ignoring him. Finally, he peered over her shoulder.

"So what's that, then?" he asked.

"You're supposed to be keeping an eye out for Cleavers," Tanith said. "That's pretty hard to do when both eyes are on me."

"I'll know when they're coming," he said, shrugging. "I'm the Terror of London, me. I know how she sounds, I know how she smells, I know how she feels. She can't keep any secrets from me. Speakin' of secrets..."

"Were we?"

"Nice little crew you've cobbled together. Vampires, killers, monsters... that Sabine girl. Everyone with their own little secrets, their own reasons for being here. All in this together. It's good. It's a good group."

Tanith knelt at an air vent, started unscrewing the grille.

"What's her deal, anyway?" Jack pressed. "Sabine, I'm talkin' about. She's not like the rest of us."

"Suppose she's not," Tanith muttered, her attention focused on the task at hand.

Jack rambled on. "She's a good one, that girl. Important to the group. She's a ray of sunshine, if I'm bein' honest. A breath of fresh air, to use an overused phrase. But that's what she is, and no mistake. A pretty little thing, but then I've always been partial to blondes. Most of the people I've killed have been blonde. Not that I'd ever harm her, of course. I'd never dream of it. Hurt somethin' so pure and so innocent? I'd rather die, I would. But she's important to the dynamic, too, you know? Can't have too many blokes on the team, am I right? We'd all start arguin' and fightin' and whatnot. Important to have some womenfolk around, like yourself and Sabine. And, to a lesser extent, Annis. I don't think anyone counts Annis, though."

Tanith looked up. "Is that what this is about? You fancy Annis?"

Jack looked genuinely horrified. "What? Where the hell did you get that from?"

"It's OK," Tanith said, getting back to work. "I won't tell her."

"I don't fancy Annis!" Jack said, his voice rising.

Tanith sighed. "Then will you please get to the point of whatever it is you're trying to say?"

He stared at her, mouth opening and closing... and then he scowled. "Nothin'," he said. "I'm sayin' nothin'."

"Then can I please get back to work? This really isn't the time or the place to start aimless conversations."

"Fine." He turned, arms folded, looking out across the city. Sulking.

Tanith rolled her eyes. Of all the possibilities she'd taken into account, she certainly hadn't expected anything like this to happen. Springheeled Jack – a lovesick puppy?

She finally got the vent unscrewed, took the glass sphere from her pocket and rolled it in. She listened to it rattle as it dropped, and then the faint sound as it broke. As she replaced the vent, she glanced over at Jack. She really didn't want to get involved in this. There was nothing she would hate more than be forced to play Cupid to these psychopathic oddballs.

"It's done," she said, standing. He grunted and she sighed. "Listen, Jack... if you have feelings for someone, I've found the best thing to do is just, you know... don't say anything."

He looked around. "Yeah?"

"Yeah. Keep it all inside. Resist the urge to make any grand romantic gesture. Or any gesture at all, in fact. Ignore her. That's the key."

"Is that how Sanguine got you?"

"No," she admitted. "He waited until I'd been possessed by a bodysnatching shadow-soul. But you... you ignore her. See how she likes that."

"Yeah," said Jack. "That might make her realise what she's missin' out on."

Tanith patted his shoulder. "I really don't care. But try it. You'd better get back now."

"You ain't comin'?"

"I've got someone to meet. I'll see you later."

Jack nodded, then hobbled away to the edge of the building and threw himself into the darkness. Tanith went east. Not even ten minutes later, she climbed through a window as Thames Chabon was sitting down for dinner.

He stared at her. A well-dressed man with a good haircut and a face you'd forget once he passed you in a crowd. There was another man in the room – a heavyset thug. Chabon's bodyguard. His hand started glowing and Tanith punched him and he hit the wall and crumpled to the floor.

"Hello, Thames," Tanith said, pulling up a chair and sitting at the table.

"Tanith Low," Chabon said, quickly regaining his composure. "Last time I saw you, you were breaking my fingers."

Tanith gave him a smile. "No, no, you're mistaken. That wasn't me, that was all Valkyrie. I just held you up."

"You're right, of course," said Thames. He started cutting into his steak. "Forgive me, I was in so much pain the details got muddled. So what can I do for you, Miss Low? Things have changed since last we met, haven't they?"

Tanith shrugged. "Such is life, I suppose. I do hope, however, that not everything has changed. You are still a purveyor of goods, aren't you? You lay your hands on things that people want – often very rare things, or... not strictly legal things."

Chabon chewed his steak and swallowed. "I've been known to break the odd law now and then, yes. Is that it? You need me to find something for you?"

"Nothing so time-consuming. I'd just like to know of your delivery methods."

"I'm sorry?"

"Thames, I know you've sourced certain items for certain mages in the London Sanctuary. I know you've delivered these items *into* the Sanctuary with the utmost secrecy. And I know you know of a hidden entrance. And that's what I need, Thames."

"Well, I'm very sorry, Miss Low, but that's a secret I intend on taking to my grave."

"Which sounds like the ideal moment for a threat, but I'm being nice."

He smiled. "And it's appreciated, be in no doubt. But that entrance is vital to my ongoing business and my ongoing well-being.

If those same mages suspected I'd betrayed them, they'd waste no time in parting me from my vital organs."

"Ah, but there is something I can do for you to make it absolutely worth your while."

"As tempting an offer as that undoubtedly is, I'm going to have to decline."

Tanith laughed. "Oh, Thames, you misunderstand. I'm keeping this entirely, one hundred percent professional. You have something I want, yes? And, as it just so happens, I have something you want."

"Which is?"

So Tanith told him what she had that he wanted so, so badly, and − she had to hand it to him – he didn't respond right away. If she hadn't known better, she could have sworn he really didn't care.

"Is that so?" Chabon murmured.

"I propose a trade," Tanith said. "You take me to the secret door into the Sanctuary, and I give you what you want. After – what, two years? – your search will finally be over."

Chabon looked at her. "Fair enough. But if you try to cheat me..."

Tanith clapped her hands delightedly. "Splendid news! Thames, I don't mind telling you, you've made me a very happy girl."

21

The room Tanith backed into was filled with cages, and in those cages, men and women stood and sat. These people were the worst of the worst, criminals of such a sickening and grotesque order that they had to be held here, in the Sanctuary itself.

The White Cleaver pursued her steadily down the steps, sparks flying as their blades clashed. The prisoners started to shout and cheer as Tanith was forced back, enemies all around her. The Cleaver's blade passed along her belly, drawing blood. She retreated under his impossibly fast onslaught, barely managing to keep up her defence.

The prisoners reached through the cage bars at her, pulling at her hair, trying to scratch her. One of them snagged her coat and she spun out of it before the Cleaver could close the gap.

He swung and she blocked with the scabbard and flicked up with the sword, but he was twisting the scythe, deflecting the strike and coming back with one of his own.

The prisoners howled with laughter as she ran to the wall, the Cleaver right behind her. She jumped to the wall and kept going till she was upside down, and she crossed the ceiling, trading blows with the Cleaver below her. He was forced to walk backwards, to defend and attack over his own head. She struck his hand with her scabbard and he dropped his scythe. She flipped to the ground, grabbed it with one hand while the other drove her sword into him.

The prisoners stopped jeering. The Cleaver took a step back.

She buried the scythe blade in his chest. He fell to his knees, black blood dripping on to the floor.

The prisoners were muttering now, cheated out of seeing her die. Tanith pulled her sword from the Cleaver's body and ran for the steps.

She heard a crash from elsewhere in the Sanctuary. The Repository. Valkyrie and Skulduggery were in trouble. Urgency lent her speed. Just as she neared the top step, however, one of the prisoners laughed.

She looked back, saw the White Cleaver standing, pulling the scythe from his body. She turned for the door again, ran the last few steps and then the breath went out of her. She looked down, at the tip of the scythe that protruded through her chest.

The Cleaver walked up the steps towards her. That was some throw. She almost laughed. Her sword fell from her grip. He took hold of the scythe. He circled, moving her around, looking at her like he was observing her pain, remembering what it was like. A twist of his hands and she was forced to her knees. She gasped when he removed the weapon. Her body was shutting down.

He raised the scythe. Tanith looked up, ready to die, but when he had circled her, he had passed through the doorway, and was now standing out in the corridor.

She lunged, slamming the door in his visored face. She pressed her hand against it and whispered, "Withstand." The sheen spread over the door just as the Cleaver began to pound on it from the other side.

Tanith tried standing but her body couldn't take any more. She slumped to the ground. The prisoners watched from their cages with delighted eyes, and as her blood seeped through her tunic, they started whispering. The whispers filled her head, slowly flooding every recess and corner of her mind. Time dragged, became something abstract. Unreal. How long had she been sitting here? How much blood was there left for her weak heart to pump through the wound?

She started crawling. Down the steps. The strength left her arms and her weight fell forward and she tumbled the rest of the way to the floor. It didn't even hurt, though. Not on any level she could feel. Those whispers blocked the pain, and she started crawling again, to the cages. There was one held off the ground, and inside it was a man with dark hair, whispering with all the others. He reached down and she reached up and his hand found hers and he pulled her, helped her to stand. He never stopped whispering. None of them did.

She pressed her hand to the lock on the cage. This wasn't an easy one. She really had to concentrate. She frowned. Bit her lip. The lock clicked. Tanith stepped back, blinked, watched the cage door open and frowned again. Had she opened it? Why had she opened it? Why would she—

Her legs gave out and she fell, but there was a man beside her and she dropped softly into his arms. It was the man from the cage, the one she'd released. He lifted her. Even if she'd wanted to struggle, she wouldn't have been able to. Her life was dripping on to the floor, robbing her of her strength. The whispers had stopped.

"I'm dying," she mumbled.

"Not if we get you medical assistance," replied the man. He carried her to the door, tried to open it, but it wouldn't budge.

She shook her head. Her thoughts were jumbled. "The White Cleaver," she said.

"He's gone by now," said the man. "Open the door."

Some part of her knew that this wasn't a good idea. Some part of her, growing quieter with every slow heartbeat. She was finding it hard to keep her thoughts in order. She reached out. He moved her closer, so she could rest her hand flat against the door. It took a few attempts, but finally, Tanith focused long enough for the door to stop shimmering. Behind her, the prisoners in the cages started laughing again. The man put her down.

"No," she said dully.

"Moribund," said another one of the prisoners, "hurry. Release us."

The man, Moribund, ignored the call. He knelt by Tanith's side.

Her mouth was dry. "You tricked me," she whispered.

"I am sorry," he said. "I was imprisoned here a long time ago. I have to escape while I can."

"Free us!" a woman demanded.

Moribund looked back at the cages. "I won't be doing that," he said.

The woman spoke again. "What are you talking about? This was our plan!"

"This was my plan," Moribund corrected.

"But it wouldn't have worked without us!"

"And for that I am grateful. But each and every one of you is a killer. Each and every one of you has claimed innocent lives before you were thrown in those cages, and were I to release you, you would go on to claim many more. No. You're staying where you are."

They stared screaming at him, cursing him, flinging threats and spittle.

Tanith tried sitting up, but Moribund laid a hand on her shoulder. "Save your strength," he said.

"I'll stop you..."

"Why would you want to?"

She gritted her teeth. "I let you out..."

"And that wasn't your fault. Who are you? What's your name?"

Tanith collapsed back. It was all she could do to keep her eyes open. "Tanith Low," she said.

Moribund nodded to her. "Tanith Low, when a sorcerer's power is bound, it doesn't disappear — it just becomes inaccessible. But there are faint dregs of magic that are still available to us. Too weak on their own, when combined with others, they can perform one single task — instil a simple command into an unsuspecting mind. Injured as you are, you were the perfect candidate. You are not to blame for releasing me, Tanith."

"I can't let you go. You're a... you're a killer like them..."

Moribund glanced back at the screaming prisoners. "I was worse," he said. "Once upon a time, I was the most evil person in this room. But I'm not that man any more. I've changed. I don't expect you to believe me. In your place, I wouldn't. But it's true, and now I have several lifetimes' worth of evil to make up for. Starting today."

He moved her, propping her up against the wall, alleviating the pain slightly. "I will send word once I'm clear of the Sanctuary," he said. "If no one has found you by then, I'll get a doctor to you. You're going to live, Tanith Low."

"And what's to stop them from... getting me to open another cage?"

"It won't work if you're aware of what's happening." He stood up. "I have to go."

"I will find you," she said.

He smiled down at her. "No, you won't. But I'll find you. I owe you a favour, and I pay my debts."

22

ane and O'Callahan returned the Gulfstream V jet to the hangar from which they'd taken it, as good as new, if you didn't count the bullet holes and rocket damage. Vex borrowed a car without asking and they drove into the City of London, and as morning broke a doctor named Brennock poked at Vex's leg with a pen. "You've been shot," he said.

Vex nodded. "I can see we've come to the right person."

"You only said *she* was shot," Brennock continued, nodding to Aurora as she sat on the bed. "You said one person with a bullet wound, not two. Definitely not two. You didn't say *you'd* been shot. This is very, very unprofessional. I have half a mind to walk out of here and leave you to your injury."

"You fixed Aurora," said Vex.

"Yes, he did," Aurora said, tapping her side. "Stings a bit, but otherwise good as new."

"She was lucky," said Brennock. "It passed right through without hitting any vital organs."

"Did any of my vital organs get hit?" Vex asked. Then, "Do legs *have* any vital organs?"

Brennock folded his arms. "You didn't tell me there were two people who needed my help."

"I thought that might have put you off. I know how reluctant you can be to leave your house."

"We're *in* my house."

"I was talking metaphorically."

"We're in my house," Brennock repeated, "and Ms Jane is getting bloodstains all over my sheets while your friends downstairs are eating all my food. I can't be seen talking to you people. Anyone who has any contact with an operative from the Irish Sanctuary has to report it, did you know that? We're to report it immediately and, if possible, delay them until the Cleavers get here."

"Grand Mage Ode must not like us."

"Well," said Brennock, a little haughtily, "you did get our last Grand Mage killed."

"Strom may have died on Irish soil," Vex said, "but it was an English blade that took his life, or has Ode forgotten that Tanith Low was the one to swing it? We're going up against her right now, for God's sake. Ode should be thanking us."

"No one mentions Low when they talk about Strom. They just talk about how he died because of the Irish Sanctuary."

"Well, that's convenient," Vex muttered.

"I could go to prison for helping you."

"It's appreciated."

"That's all? That's all you're going to say?"

"It's... *really* appreciated?"

"What about compensation for the risk I'm taking?"

"I could give you a hug."

"I'm talking about money!"

"You can't put a price on hugs."

"You're making jokes? You're making jokes while you're putting my life in danger?"

"Oh, your life's not in danger."

"They could execute me for harbouring fugitives."

"We're not fugitives. We haven't committed any crime that they're aware of. If anything, you'd be executed for aiding the enemy during a time of near-war. So that'd be treason."

"Oh my God."

"Brennock, we appreciate the risk you're taking in helping us.

We do. But I'm not going to pay you because that would cheapen both of us. Besides, you owe me. Who introduced you to your wife?"

Brennock frowned. "A mutual friend."

"Ah, but who introduced you to your mutual friend?"

"My brother."

"My point, Brennock, is that if you go far enough back into your past, I'm sure you'll find someone with a link to me. Or at least to Saracen. He gets around."

"I do," Saracen agreed as he poked his head in. "Gracious is back."

Vex looked at Brennock. "Doc, seriously. Fix me."

Brennock hesitated, then scowled. His hands started glowing, radiating heat. "Try not to move," he said, and placed his hands over the wound. The heat intensified and Vex gritted his teeth.

Aurora slid off the bed and went downstairs, but Saracen stayed, and peered closer. "What are you doing?"

"Disintegrating the bullet shards," Brennock mumbled.

The heat spread and Vex was sure he could feel his skin starting to blister. And then it was over, and Brennock took his hands away and coolness rushed in.

"It's already started to heal," Brennock said, dabbing the wound with ointment. He wrapped Vex's leg with a bandage and gave him a pouch of leaves. "Chew one every hour," he instructed. "It'll be fine, so long as you don't get shot in the same place."

"You're a good man, Doc," said Vex. He put his weight on his leg and it wasn't bad at all.

"You'll be leaving now, I expect?"

"Absolutely," said Vex. "Leaving soon, anyway. As soon as it gets dark."

"You're spending the *day* here?"

"Ah, you're very kind. Thank you. But I have to insist, the moment night falls we are *gone*. Midnight at the very latest."

Brennock glowered. "In that case, I think I shall go for a very long walk."

"Probably wise."

Brennock left and Vex joined the others in the kitchen. By the time he got there he wasn't even limping any more.

"Dexter," said Gracious, "I was just telling the others here – I talked to my friend. He says there have been no recent disturbances inside the Sanctuary."

Vex nodded. "Hopefully that means Tanith hasn't broken in yet. Which means she's going in tonight, and so are we. This friend of yours – do you think he'll be able to let us in?"

"Not without getting himself arrested. But don't worry, I have a few tricks up my sleeve that I've been working on. You leave it to me."

"Fair enough," said Vex. "But I have to admit, now I'm slightly nervous. Whatever you have planned, keep in mind that we need to be stealthy. In and out without making anyone suspicious. It's going to be risky, and if we're caught, we're going to prison. Or we're going to get killed. So anyone who thinks they have better things to do on a Saturday night, now is the time to walk away."

No one moved. No one spoke. Until Saracen leaned in towards Aurora.

"We might die tonight."

She glared at him, then shrugged. "Help me up."

He took her hand and they walked out, and Gracious hung his head.

There'd been all kinds of plans for how to sneak into the Sanctuary, but each one was discarded because either it wasn't very good or it wasn't very possible. In the end, they just walked up to the side door and knocked.

The door opened and the Administrator, Merriwyn Hyphenate-Bash, looked out. Her gaze took them all in, and then settled on Frightening.

"Mr Jones," she said, "I wasn't aware of an appointment."

"No appointment," said Frightening, "but I need to gain entry nonetheless."

"I'm sorry, sir, but security has been tightened and rules must be obeyed. If you'd like, I could have a representative of the Council come outside to meet with you, and if he is satisfied, we can begin formal procedures to get you a temporary visitor's pass."

"What do you make of this?" Gracious asked, stepping forward and handing her a small glass cube.

Once it was in Merriwyn's hand, it started glowing. "It's certainly very pretty," she said, gazing at the colours. "Where did you find it?"

"It was just over there," said Gracious, "I thought someone might have dropped it. The lights are interesting, aren't they? Almost hypnotic."

Merriwyn nodded. "Very pretty indeed."

"They'd almost put you to sleep, wouldn't they? If you look at them hard enough."

"They might very well do."

"You can almost feel your eyelids getting heavier..."

"I suppose you're right."

"Look at all the nice colours..."

"I'm looking."

"Feel yourself getting more and more tired..."

"I'm not really tired, though."

"Feel your eyelids starting to droop..."

Vex sighed as Gracious toppled over in a deep, deep sleep.

"Oh, my," was all Merriwyn had time to say before Aurora punched her and she collapsed into Frightening's arms.

Donegan nudged Gracious in the face with his foot until his partner moaned and sat up. "That," Donegan said, "was brilliant. You have outdone yourself, Gracious, you really have."

Gracious blinked sleepily. "Did it work?"

"You're a genius," said Donegan. "A magical, mystical genius. They'll write songs about you in years to come. They won't be any good, these songs, and they'll mostly be out of tune and have a lot of humming, but they'll be songs, and that's the important thing."

Vex helped Gracious to his feet and they all slipped through the door.

"Two Cleavers in the next room," Saracen whispered. "Both of them facing us."

"I'll handle this," said Gracious.

Aurora frowned. "Are you sure?"

Gracious waved away her concerns, and took a red rubber ball from his pocket.

"They're not puppies," Donegan reminded him.

"Everybody shield your eyes," Gracious said as he squeezed the ball a few times, bounced it and then lobbed it through the doorway. Vex looked away just before a bright flash lit up everything.

Silence. No alarms raised.

Gracious crept to the door and looked out. Finally, he breathed in relief. "It worked."

Vex and the others followed him out. Two Cleavers stood perfectly still.

Frightening approached one slowly, waving his hand in front of the visor. "What did you do to them?"

"They're on sensory shutdown," said Gracious. "They'll come to in a few minutes with no idea that anything weird happened."

"Sensory shutdown? OK, that sounds fine. But are you sure you haven't just wiped their brains?"

"Pretty sure," said Gracious. "I mean, yeah, it's a risk, but... No, they're fine. My calculations were correct. This isn't the first time I've used this, and the test subject showed no signs of impaired cognitive ability."

"Who was the test subject?" asked Aurora.

"I test everything out on myself before taking it into the field."

She stared at him. "You zapped your own brain?"

"And it didn't do me any harm apart from the dizziness and the vomiting spells and the weirdly persistent ringing in my ears. Also the blackouts and the mood swings and the creeping paranoia. Apart from that, zero side effects, if you don't count numb fingertips. Which I don't."

"Because he also lost the ability to count," said Donegan.

"That was temporary," snapped Gracious. "We're in, aren't we?"

"Yes, we are," said Vex. "And now we need to get to the sword without encountering any mages or Cleavers. Saracen? Think you can guide us?"

"Sure," said Saracen, and closed his eyes. He swivelled his head slowly, and then pointed. His eyes opened. "This way."

23

"How long before they're in position?"

Sanguine glanced at his watch. "A little under five minutes."

Jack nodded, and looked out over the city. "Beautiful here."

"Cold."

"Well, you would say that, wouldn't you? You're from warmer climes. You're soft."

"Is that so?"

"Of course it is," said Tanith, approaching from behind. "You're a Texas boy. You're used to being pampered by the sun. In London, we've got to be that little bit tougher, don't we, Jack?"

"Indeed we do," Jack answered, and he hobbled to the edge of the roof.

"How long have you been around, anyway?" Sanguine asked Jack.

"Me? Don't know, really. Don't remember bein' a kid. Don't remember family or nothin'. I can remember the last few hundred years, and then things go foggy. I remember bits and pieces from before that, but..." He shrugged. "For all I know, I've always been alive, but I'm only able to remember the last few centuries."

"You might be lucky," said Sanguine. "I remember every little detail about my childhood, and I wish I didn't."

"At least you know where you came from."

Sanguine grunted, didn't say anything.

"And at least you're not alone," Jack continued. "As long as you keep those sunglasses on, no one's ever gonna look at you and think anythin' is out of the ordinary. But me? All I *am* is out of the ordinary."

Sanguine stayed where he was while Tanith joined Jack by the edge. "Maybe if you left London a little bit more," she said, "maybe travelled the world, you could have found more like you."

Jack gave a little laugh. "That's assumin' that there *are* others like me. I know you say you've got all this super secret information on what I am, but I've come to the conclusion a long time ago: I'm the only one of my kind, and my time is runnin' out. One of these days I'm gonna make the wrong move or take on the wrong victim and then no more me. And when I die, my species dies."

Tanith folded her arms against the cold. "Ever think about settling down? Maybe try raising a few springheeled kiddies? They wouldn't be pure-blood, but that'd probably be for the best, if I'm being honest."

"Sure," said Jack, "no problem. Because I got scores of women linin' up for the chance to settle down with me."

"You don't need scores," said Tanith. "You just need one."

"Yeah? You offerin'?"

"Not me," she laughed. "But maybe I know one who might be interested. Maybe you do too."

Jack hesitated, like he didn't want to appear too eager. "I... I have had my eye on someone."

"Have you told her?"

"What? You told me the best thing was not to say anything. To ignore her."

"I did?" said Tanith, frowning. "Oh, yeah. Well, I was busy. I really just wanted you to shut up."

Jack sighed. "Anyway, what would I say? You're a pretty little thing – do you want to spend the rest of your life with me?"

Sanguine couldn't stop himself. "Pretty?" he echoed.

Jack whipped his head round. "Don't you even *think* about insultin' her."

Sanguine held up his hands. "No, no, hey, whatever floats your boat, man. Far as I'm concerned, Tanith's got the prettiest face in all the land..."

"Aw, thank you," said Tanith.

"... followed closely by that China Sorrows."

Tanith scowled.

"But yeah," he continued, "I suppose, in her own way, Annis is a pretty little thing."

Jack stared at him. "What?"

"She might be in need of a bath, and a hairbrush, some moisturiser and maybe some light cosmetic surgery, but slap a new dress on her, nothing too revealing or tight, and you'd have... well, you'd have a short, squat woman in a dress. Which is great, if that's what you're after."

"I don't fancy Black Annis."

"OK then, you love her, whatever."

"I don't love Black Annis! Why does everyone think I love Black Annis?"

Tanith frowned at Jack. "OK, I don't understand. Who have we been talking about?"

"Sabine!"

"Sabine? You and Sabine? *You?* And *Sabine?*"

Jack's face burned, and he turned away. "I know it's ridiculous. Beautiful young woman like her. Ugly old freak like me."

"It *is* fairly ridiculous," Sanguine agreed.

"The heart wants what the heart wants," Tanith said, patting Jack's shoulder.

Jack shook his head. "I'm a fool. I'm deludin' myself, is what I'm doing. Look at me. Why would anyone as pretty as her want anythin' to do with me? And I try to be charmin' and witty when she's around and I just come off as... I dunno."

"Desperate?" said Sanguine. "Sad? Pathetic?"

"Yeah. All those things. I repulse her. She looks at me and her stomach turns. She talks to me and all she wants to do is walk away. I'll never get her. I'm destined to be alone for the rest of my miserable life."

"You know what she told me?" Tanith said. "She said she's on the lookout for a new man. She said she's bored of the type she usually dates — she wants someone a bit... different."

"I'm different, all right."

"She said she doesn't care about looks," Tanith said. "All she wants is someone to make her laugh. Can you make her laugh, Jack?"

"I... I think so."

"Because you know something else? When she was saying all this to me, her eyes kept drifting over to you."

"Seriously?"

"Seriously."

Jack went quiet. Sanguine imagined that he could see the hope blossom deep within him, and Jack stood a bit straighter, and held his head up a bit higher, so that when Tanith swung her sword, the head came cleanly off without the need for any hacking.

The body crumpled and the head bounced beside it, losing the top hat as it came rolling to a gentle stop.

"I could have done it," said Sanguine. "Didn't have to be you."

Tanith shrugged and wiped the blood from her blade. "Seemed only fair that I be the one," she said. "Did you like the bit about Sabine maybe fancying him?"

"I did. Thought it was a really sweet thing to do for him in his last moments."

"Yeah," said Tanith, "that's me all over. Give me sixty seconds to get to the others, then dump his body over the side."

She jumped off the roof and disappeared.

Sanguine moved the body to the very edge and waited. When the sixty seconds were up, he counted out fifteen more, just to be generous, then nudged the body over the edge with his foot. The body of Springheeled Jack fell clumsily, with none of the grace he had displayed when he used to dance across rooftops.

It hit the street far below in a wet, tangled mess of limbs and broken bones, and from where he stood Sanguine could hear the screams of passers-by. He kicked the head off after it, and picked up the top hat and threw it into the wind.

24

anith waited until the last of the sentries had run to investigate the source of all the screaming, then slipped out from hiding. She moved quickly down a narrow street, saw Thames Chabon and three of his men running up from the other side. They met in the middle beside a large metal rubbish skip and he tapped the wall.

"This is what we call the tradesman's entrance," he said. "It'll take you into a storeroom. There's never anyone in there. What you do next is not my concern."

Tanith examined the wall. "How does it open?"

"It doesn't," said Chabon. "You stand here, activate the

mechanism, and you turn intangible for three seconds. In those three seconds you walk straight through."

"How do I activate the mechanism?"

"Sorry, not sharing that little secret. I'll activate it for you, once you give me my payment. How you get out again, that's up to you."

"I have that covered," she said. "Please stand back, I don't want you to spook my associates."

Once Chabon and his men stepped behind the skip, Tanith took out her phone, pressed SEND. Moments later, Sabine ran up, followed by Annis and Wilhelm. Dusk came last. His fists were clenched and he was sweating. His body trembled. Following Tanith's instruction, he hadn't taken his serum, and he was fighting the change. Tanith kept an eye on him.

"Where is it?" Wilhelm asked, fear in his voice. "Where's the door? You said you'd be meeting your contact. Where is he?"

"Wilhelm," Tanith said, "calm down."

"The sentries will be back at any moment! They'll find us! They'll arrest us, or kill us! We have to run!"

Sabine stepped up to him, slapped him hard across the face. He stared at her in shock.

"Stop panicking," Sabine said.

"OK," he mumbled.

Sabine looked at Tanith. "Do you know how we get in?"

"I do."

"Then what are we waiting for?"

"I just have to pay the man," Tanith said, and watched how wide Sabine's eyes got when Chabon's men grabbed her from behind.

"Hello, Sabine," said Chabon as she struggled. "Did you really think you'd be able to avoid me forever?"

"Tanith," said Sabine, "please, help me, he'll kill me—"

"That's the risk you take when you con a gangster," Tanith told her. "Mr Chabon, activate the mechanism and our business will be concluded."

"Tanith, no!" Sabine cried. "Annis, do something!"

Black Annis sniffed. "Maybe this'll teach you not to steal other women's men."

"What? What the hell are you...? Wilhelm! Dusk! Help me!"

Wilhelm stared at his shoes, and Dusk didn't seem to even notice Sabine's predicament, so preoccupied was he with his own discomfort.

"Take her to the van," Chabon said. His men dragged Sabine backwards, covering her mouth to silence her screams. The last Tanith saw of her, her eyes were wide and full of fear and then she vanished in the shadows.

"Group together," said Chabon, "and face the wall. On the count of three, you walk forward quickly. Very quickly, do you understand? If you become solid halfway through, it'll be messy."

Tanith faced the wall. Chabon was somewhere behind them. She fought the urge to peek. Knowing how to sneak in here would be very handy indeed.

"Three," Chabon said, "two, one. Go."

A light hit them from somewhere and Tanith's entire body buzzed. She held her hand up to the wall and she could see the bricks through it. It was the hand of a ghost – pale and slightly luminescent. She walked forward, forcing herself to keep her eyes open as she passed through the wall, almost laughing at the sensation. Then she was on the other side, in a dimly lit room, and she returned to normal.

"Everyone in one piece?" she asked.

Wilhelm was frantically searching himself to make sure he was OK. Annis didn't bother, and Dusk didn't care. He winced in pain, and Tanith saw how jagged his teeth had become. They were splitting his gums and filling his mouth. It wouldn't be long now.

"I thought we were a team," Annis said.

Tanith looked down at her. "We are a team."

"And Sabine? Wasn't she part of it, too?"

"She was a very important part of it. She was payment."

"Are you going to betray us like you betrayed her?"

"No," said Tanith, "of course not. Sabine didn't belong here and you know it. She's not like us. But we needed her, and now that she's gone, the rest of us can forge ahead. You. Me. Dusk. Sanguine. Even Wilhelm here."

"And Jack," said Annis.

Tanith nodded. "Of course. And Jack. The team wouldn't be the team without Jack. Come on, we don't have much time."

She knew this Sanctuary well, so she led them through the corridors nobody used, ducking into empty rooms to avoid Cleaver patrols. The closer they got to the Repository, though, the harder it was to stay unnoticed. Still, their luck held much longer than she thought it would. They were actually in sight of the Repository door before three sorcerers stumbled upon them.

The sorcerers stared, then backed away.

"Dusk," Tanith said softly as the sorcerers turned and ran.

Dusk took off in pursuit, low to the ground, almost loping after them. He pulled at his chest and his skin parted instantly and the vampire bounded from Dusk's human form. It disappeared round the corner, already closing the distance between it and its prey.

"Let's go," Tanith said. "Before it comes back for us."

They ran to the door, slipped in and closed it after them. The Repository was massive. Books and magical items lined the shelves, some open to display, some held behind unbreakable glass. The sword was in a case at the back of the room, and Tanith led the others straight to it and a voice said—

"I wouldn't take one more step if I were you."

Tanith turned slowly, smiling at Vex and the others as they stood there looking all cool. She waited for the Cleavers to pounce, and when they didn't, her smile widened.

"They don't know you're here, do they?" she said. "No one knows. Look at us. Peas in a pod, aren't we? We break in here, you break in here. We want to steal the sword, you want to steal the sword. A merry old time had by all."

"There is a difference, though," said Vex. "There are six of us, and only three of you."

"Yeah," Tanith said, "but somewhere in this Sanctuary, we have a vampire."

"Which would slaughter you as soon as it would slaughter us," said Saracen. "Hello, Tanith. You're looking well."

"Saracen Rue and Frightening Jones," said Tanith. "Two ex-boyfriends. And Aurora. Hi, Aurora. And all of you wanting to kill me. This isn't good for my self-esteem, you know."

"We're not here to kill you," said Frightening. "We're here to stop you. To bring you in, if we can."

"So they can cure me? I don't need to be cured. Look at me. Do I not look happy? I think everyone just needs to take a step

233

back, relax, and accept that this is the new me. I'm just like the old me, but better."

"You're not getting the sword," said Vex. "We'd destroy it before we let you get your hands on it."

Her laugh was so sudden and so genuine that it actually made Vex frown, and she said, "Well, if I had known that earlier, I could have just stayed at home!"

"Wait," he said, "so you're *destroying* the weapons, that's what you're doing?"

Tanith grinned. "Of course. You want to use them to kill Darquesse, and I want to melt them down to slag before she even turns up. I've seen the future. I've seen what she becomes. People like you, you're going to need God-Killer weapons just to get her to notice you."

"And the rest of your little gang?" Saracen said, looking at Annis and Wilhelm. "I can understand why Tanith wants the world to end – she's got a Remnant living inside her – but what about you, Annis?"

"I've lived in this world for over two hundred years," Annis said, mumbling slightly. "Haven't made one friend. No one's ever loved me, no one's ever cared for me. It won't be so bad, seeing the world being burnt to a cinder."

"Wilhelm?" said Vex. "You can't tell me you want to die."

Wilhelm licked his lips. "I just... I don't want to die, no, but...

But if I do this, I get my reward. We all get our rewards. I'm really sorry about, you know, about being a traitor and everything, but it was an offer I couldn't turn down..."

"Don't apologise," said Tanith. "It's boring. Become one with your spineless nature, Wilhelm. It's the only way people will like you."

"Tanith Low," said Vex, "you're under arrest."

"You can't arrest me from all the way over there."

"What do you say we meet in the middle?"

"I can do that," Tanith said, grinning as she went for her sword.

And then the alarm went off.

25

Heavy doors slammed shut, alarms wailed and all around them Cleavers were appearing. Mages burst from a hidden tunnel, hands and eyes glowing with power, flames burning in their palms. It was a trap. It was a trap and they'd all walked right into it.

"Nobody," said a narrow man as he approached, "move."

Vex looked at the others, making sure they weren't about to do something stupid. Then he looked at Tanith and her gang. Annis was whipping her head around, eyes wide in alarm, but as yet her skin wasn't turning blue, so that was a good sign. Wilhelm shrieked, of course, and Tanith stayed calm, a slightly mocking smile on her face.

The narrow man's name was Palaver Graves. When Grand Mage Strom had been killed, Cothernus Ode moved up to take his place, and Graves in turn had stepped in to fill Ode's place as an Elder. Vex hadn't had much to do with him over the years, had met him once or twice, but had no idea if he liked him or not.

"Look at all you pesky little flies," said Graves slowly, enjoying the moment, "all trapped helplessly in my web."

Yeah, Vex was pretty sure he didn't like this guy.

"Dexter Vex," said Graves. "Saracen Rue. Gracious O'Callahan. Three Irish mages breaking into the English Sanctuary to steal a weapon of unstoppable power... some might say that is reason enough to go to war."

"This has nothing to do with the Irish Sanctuary," said Saracen. "We're here on our own behalf."

"Yes, yes," Graves said, "you would say that, wouldn't you? And who do you have with you? Frightening Jones, operative from the largest Sanctuary in Africa. Donegan Bane, rogue English mage."

"I'm a rogue," said Donegan, sounding pleased.

"And Aurora Jane," Graves finished, "an American mage who has betrayed her own Sanctuary. You should all be ashamed of yourselves."

Aurora nodded. "I've decided," she said. "I don't like you."

Vex looked at her. "That's exactly what I was thinking."

"And me," said Frightening.

"Me, too," said Tanith.

"Ah, yes," Graves said, switching his attention to the other group, "and here we have the infamous Tanith Low. Now then, is this the corrupted evil killer version, or do you still have the Remnant inside you?"

He chuckled at his little joke. Tanith smiled, but said nothing.

"It's been fun," Graves said, "watching you all sneak in, all stealthy and quiet. Obviously, we've been expecting you since Johann Starke reported the dagger missing eight hours ago. Once we heard of the trouble in Chicago, we reasoned that it was only a matter of time before the thief, or thieves, would try to add the sword to their collection. I have to admit, however, having two sets of rival robbers fall into my trap at the same time, well... that was an unexpected bonus."

This time, Tanith laughed.

"I'm so glad you find this as amusing as I do," said Graves, laughing along with her.

"More amusing, actually."

"Oh, I doubt it."

"No, really," said Tanith. "I'd say I'm far more amused at this moment than you could possibly be."

Annoyance dimmed the smile on Graves's face. "And why is that? Are you amused by your own stupidity? Are you amused

238

by the prospect of spending the rest of your miserable life in a prison cell with your powers bound?"

"Nope," Tanith said. "I'm just amused at your definition of a trap, that's all."

Graves made a point of looking at all of his mages and Cleavers before looking back at her. "You're surrounded," he said. "Outgunned. Outmatched. Outmanoeuvred."

"But not outsmarted."

"Is that so? You think you're smarter than me, is that it? You're a thug, Miss Low. Oh, yes, I know all about you. You were trained as an assassin, then diversified into mercenary activities, before finding yourself as a freelance bounty hunter. You like to fight. That's all you like to do. Whereas I am a scholar. I have dedicated my life to the languages of magic. I have peeled back secrets and explored hidden truths."

"Doesn't make you smarter than me," Tanith said. "Just more boring."

Graves's patience was wearing thin, and it was showing on his face. "Throw down your weapons and put your hands in the air. And somebody turn that bloody siren off, it's giving me a headache."

Tanith grinned, but did as she was told, laying her sword on the ground. Gracious and Donegan surrendered their guns. The Cleavers swarmed, shackles at the ready, and a moment later the wailing ceased and the heavy doors opened. Vex held out his hands for a shiny set of shackles, but there was a scuffle across the room, and he glimpsed Tanith kicking someone. He looked at the Cleaver in front, the one with the shackles. At the last moment he shoved the Cleaver away from him and backed up, aware that Saracen and the others had done exactly the same thing. Now they stood in a tight pack, tense, watching the Cleavers and mages around them, everyone waiting for the spark that would ignite the battle.

"This is ridiculous!" Graves shouted. "You don't stand a chance! None of you do!"

Vex could see Tanith now through the throng of Cleavers, grinning again.

"Tanith Low," Graves said, his voice practically quivering with indignation, "you will allow the Cleaver to shackle you or I will give the order to—"

"Ask me how smart I am," Tanith said.

"What?"

"Ask me," she said. "Go on. I dare you."

He glared at her. "Very well. Miss Low, how smart are you?"

"Very," she told him. "I've always been a pretty smart cookie, even before the Remnant. I was no genius, mind you. But I was pretty smart. Smart enough to get by, you know? But the Remnant, well... the Remnant has been in some pretty sharp minds, let me tell you, not least of which was one Kenspeckle Grouse. You heard of him?"

"Yes," Graves said, actually rolling his eyes. "The professor of science-magic. Died a few years ago."

"That's the one," said Tanith. "So while I'm not *technically* as smart as he was, at the same time, I've lived in his head. I have all of his memories tucked away in mine. For instance, the memory of how to concoct a certain virus in gaseous form, place it into an itty-bitty glass sphere and dump it into the ventilation system of a certain building."

No one was bothering with Vex and the others any more. Everyone was looking at Tanith.

"What... what kind of virus?" Graves asked.

"Ever see that movie *28 Days Later*, with Cillian Murphy and Brendan Gleeson? You know those rage-zombies that ran everywhere?"

Graves swallowed. "Yes?"

"Good movie, isn't it? It was on TV there a few weeks ago. Gave me the idea. A rage virus in a gas, pumped through the ventilation ducts. That's what I did."

Graves hesitated, then smiled. Then laughed. "So you've infected us all with a rage virus, have you? So we're all mindless rage-zombies, screaming and tearing each other apart, yes? Well, that *is* impressive. Although I do seem to be remarkably calm for a rage-zombie, don't I? As does everyone else here. I wonder why that is? Maybe, and this is just a suggestion, maybe it's because you're really not as smart as you think you are?"

"Maybe," Tanith said. "Or maybe because I know the protocol of this place I've been able to anticipate every move you've made so far."

Graves laughed again. "Such as?"

"Such as the lockdown," said Tanith. "When the Sanctuary is breached, the entire building goes into lockdown mode, where corridors are sealed off and certain areas get air pumped in from new sources. And then, once the lockdown is called off, all these people in those areas who have been exposed to this air are free to roam."

Graves was starting to look decidedly pale.

"We're not the ones infected," said Tanith. "But if you listen closely, I'm pretty sure you'll be able to hear the ones that are."

And just as if it had all been rehearsed, Vex could now hear people screaming and shouting, and getting closer.

Graves spun to the mage behind him. "Lock it down," he commanded. "Now. Immediately. Lock everything down!"

"He can't do that," Tanith said calmly. "It takes twenty-three minutes for the lockdown cycle to complete. So we've got roughly twenty minutes to go before those doors can close again. Think you can survive for twenty minutes, Mr Graves?"

From where he stood, Vex could see the door. It was dark out in the corridor, where the screaming was coming from, but he could make out shapes. Moving fast. Moving fast.

"Get ready," he said. "Here they come."

26

hey came screaming through the doors, sorcerers and Cleavers fighting each other, then swarming the room. The unaffected sorcerers backed away at first, but with no other choice and nowhere to run, they started fighting back. Those the gas had affected, the rage-zombies, weren't bothering with magic or tactics – all they seemed to want to do was get their hands on someone and tear them to pieces.

A man came at Tanith and she sent him flying. A Cleaver grabbed her arm and she stomped on his knee and shoved him into another mage. Whether they were contorted with anger or fear, all these faces were starting to look the same. She glimpsed

Vex and Saracen and the others on the other side of the room, hitting whoever got close. Vex looked up, locked eyes with Tanith. She grinned at him.

He ran for the God-Killer, but she was faster, running up the wall and over the heads of the fighting, biting, snarling masses. Black Annis was already turning blue, her nails and teeth growing, and she launched herself into the mix, adding to the chaos. Not even the Cleavers' scythes could scratch that blue hide, and her matted, greying hair swung heavily about her terrifying face as she got to work.

Tanith landed by the glass case and Vex grabbed her, hauled her away. She spun, crunching an elbow into his ribs. He grunted but held on, managed to send her stumbling. Before she fell, she got a hand to the ground, cartwheeled to her feet again as he rushed in. His first punch missed, his second caught her, and then a right cross sent her stumbling. Lucky shot.

She wiped blood from her lip, and grinned at him. "I like your shoes," she said.

She sprang at him, brought him down. He squirmed beneath her, shifting his hips and pressing his knee to her stomach. Her hands closed round his throat. Tightened. She liked being strong. He pushed with his knee, but she held on, squeezing tighter, and then he let her fall into him as he sent a palm shot into her chin. Lights danced before her eyes and when her brain came back online, she was face down and Vex was on her back with his arm round her throat. How the hell had that happened?

Out of the corner of her eye she saw people running, then Vex was lifted off her by a kick accompanied by a screech, and hands were on her, pulling her up, those hands going for her eyes now, clawing at her face. Tanith's forehead crunched into the nose of the rage-zombie and he howled, and she did it again and he staggered away. A woman reached for her and Tanith kicked at her knee and her ribs and her head, the kicks tapping out a rapid rhythm that dropped the woman on the spot.

Behind her, Vex was ducking under a wild swing. He grabbed his assailant, flipped him over his hip, stamped on his groin to keep him out of the fight. Tanith backed up to him and there they stood, taking down the rage-zombies as they ran up. Tanith spun and kicked and headbutted. Vex flipped and choked and subdued. He evidently didn't want to permanently hurt anyone if he could help it. Tanith had no such qualms.

A Cleaver jumped for her and she dodged, nudging him towards Vex, who saw the scythe with barely enough time to duck. He spared a moment to glare at her and she spared a moment to grin back, and then more rage-zombies descended on them and there was a lot more punching and kicking and the breaking of arms, noses, jaws, ribs... Her heart hammered and her pulse pounded and her blood rushed through her exhilarated body.

Her smile was black-lipped and her face was black-veined and her blonde hair whipped as she fought, and it was a good day to be alive and it was a good day to hurt people.

And then she looked up, into the big black eyes of a vampire, and her smile went away.

It sprang and she somersaulted over its head, its claws ripping across her back. It crashed into a group of rage-zombies behind her, sank its teeth into a neck as its claws lacerated those around it. Tanith bit her lip against the pain, feeling the blood run down to the waistband of her trousers. She didn't take it personally. Dusk had no control over his vampire side. The creature hadn't attacked her because of who she was, it had just attacked because she was obviously a very delicious meal. Juicy, even.

"How long do the effects last?" Vex asked, at her side again, using a fistful of energy to blast a sorcerer back.

Tanith waited until a snarling mage was close enough, then kicked him in the face. "Ten minutes or so," she said, watching him twirl and fall. "Or until they're unconscious. Whichever comes first."

Someone stumbled into them and they both shoved him back into the crowd.

"Look at us," Tanith said, "sworn enemies, but fighting side by side."

"Sometimes it's better the devil you know," Vex grunted.

"It is, isn't it," she said, flashing him a bright smile.

Vex slammed an elbow into a sorcerer's jaw and Tanith slid away from a grab and brought the ridge of her hand into the throat of another attacker. She backed up once again to Vex.

There was a lull in the action, as if everyone around them had decided to ignore them for a moment, and Tanith seized her chance. She turned, swung a punch just as Vex did the same. Her fist hit him and his fist hit her and the world tilted and she was falling, banging her head on some unconscious person's knee.

Her vision swam. Everything sounded so very far away. She looked up at the high ceiling and thought of nothing. A Cleaver sent another Cleaver stumbling over her, but she didn't mind that. It wasn't the first time two men had fought over her.

The little joke made her smile, and then a worried face came into view.

"Tanith? Tanith, are you dead?"

Wilhelm. Looking scared. As usual.

He shook her. "Tanith? Please don't be dead. Please don't be dead."

"My eyelids are blinking and I'm looking at you," she mumbled. "Generally speaking, dead people don't do either of those things."

"Oh, thank God," he said, and babbled some more as he pulled her to her feet.

Her legs were shaky, but her strength was returning fast. That was some punch Vex had caught her with. Vex himself was on the ground beside them, trying his best to get up.

"Kick him," Tanith said.

Wilhelm's eyes widened. "Me? I'm not, I'm not a fighter, Tanith. I told you. I wouldn't know how to—"

"Just kick him," she said. "In the face. Before he stands up. Now, Wilhelm. *Now*."

Looking like he might cry, Wilhelm gave a half-hearted kick to Vex's leg.

"The *face*," Tanith repeated.

Wilhelm pressed his foot against Vex's ear and tried to sort of shoo him away. Tanith growled, pulled Wilhelm to one side and kicked Vex in the jaw. He slumped.

"Don't look at me like that," Wilhelm said. "I told you I'm not a fighter. I told you I shouldn't be here. I don't even know why you brought me!"

She took his hand and led him to the glass case. "Because you're very important to me, Wilhelm. Your uncle was the man who installed the security for the sword, did you know that?"

Despite his fear, Wilhelm frowned. "He was?"

"Oh, yes. Recognise that?" She pointed to the image carved into the side of the case. "That's your family crest, isn't it? The only people who can open this case are the Elders of this

Sanctuary and the man who made the case itself – or someone of his blood."

"I can open it?" Wilhelm asked, his voice breathy with wonder.

"Yes. Sort of. When I say 'of his blood', I literally mean... well..."

Keeping hold of his hand, she took her own sword from its scabbard and cut off his little finger. Wilhelm screamed and howled and fell to his knees and she left him to his distress. Holding the finger by the knuckle, she smeared a bloody symbol over the family crest and watched the crest start to glow. Something clicked, and the case opened.

Tanith tossed Wilhelm his finger – getting not even a thank you in return – and slid her sword into the scabbard across her back. Then she lifted the God-Killer from its velvet cushion. It was heavy. It was big. The blade itself was longer than she was. A ridiculously cool-looking sword, in the hands of a ridiculously cool-looking chick.

That grin was back on her face again.

A Cleaver ran at her and she swung. The sword was clumsy and awkward and the Cleaver managed to dodge all but the tip. But this was a God-Killer weapon – whatever it cut, it killed. The tip sliced through the Cleaver's coat and inflicted what would have been a nick with any other blade. But here, that nick became a swathe, and sheared his body in two.

"Wow," Tanith said.

She swung again, killing three people in one go. This time, it was almost like their torsos parted before the blade even touched them. Now *that* was sharp.

She saw the Monster Hunters move through the crowd of rage-zombies like a lawnmower moves through grass, cutting down everything in front of them. They fought as a partnership, watching the other's back. Sometimes Bane would finish off O'Callahan's opponent and sometimes O'Callahan would finish off Bane's. Saracen and Aurora were fighting alongside Graves's men, and Graves himself was being protected by Frightening. What a team.

Tanith's team, or what remained of it, wasn't doing so well. The vampire was killing everyone around it, Wilhelm was still shrieking about one teeny-tiny severed finger and Black Annis was lying dead on the floor. Her blue skin had remained unbreakable, but the business end of a scythe had found its way into her huge gaping mouth, the curving blade piercing her brain from beneath. Poor dead Annis. Tanith doubted anyone would mourn her passing. Tanith certainly wouldn't.

She ran up a wall, across the ceiling and out of the door. She flipped to the ground and kept going, pulling her phone from her pocket and dialling.

"I have it," she said. "Now would be a good time to come rescue me."

Sanguine said, "Activate your GPS and I'll ride in on a white horse."

"My hero," she said, and hung up. A few moments later, fresh alarms began to wail as the Sanctuary's defence systems picked up someone burrowing through the ground. After another few moments, she frowned. It shouldn't be taking this long. She checked her phone, made sure the GPS was sending out its signal, and then Sanguine erupted from the floor in front of her in a spray of rock and dirt, out of control and cursing as he bounced off a wall and stumbled to his knees.

"That," Tanith said, "was not as cool an entrance as you might think."

"They put something down there," he said, anger biting at his words as he stood. "I got close and all of a sudden I'm being chased. Something nipping at my heels. Something else coming to cut me off. Didn't see what they were, but they're big, and fast, and able to do what I can do."

"Can we get out?"

"*I* could make it, maybe, keep ahead of them, but two of us? No."

She chewed her lip. "Damn."

He looked around. "Just you, then?"

"Annis is dead, Dusk's on the loose and Wilhelm is still screaming," Tanith said. "Pretty much exactly how I thought it'd go."

"That's a big damn sword."

"Yes, it is." She held it out to him. "Take it. Get it out of here."

"Excuse me?"

"I'll find my own way out. Take this to the other weapons and melt them all down."

"I am not leaving you here."

"Billy-Ray," she said, looking into his sunglasses, "trust me. I'll be right behind you. But the important thing, the really important thing, is this sword. It's the dagger and the bow and the spear. They have to be destroyed – now, while we have the chance."

"There is no way I'm leaving without you. We had a plan. We stick to the plan."

"The plan didn't take into account whatever is in the ground waiting for you."

"Then we don't leave through the ground. We leave through the walls. You think any more alarm bells ringing is gonna make a difference to anyone? We just walk out of here."

"Too much could go wrong."

"Tanith—"

She cut him off. "Billy-Ray, that's the new plan, OK? That's what we're doing. You get out of here now, right now, and you destroy the God-Killers. I'll make my own way out and meet up with you."

"Damn it, woman—"

She grabbed him, kissed him, pressed the God-Killer into his hands and stepped back.

He looked at her. "Will you marry me?"

"What?"

"This might not be the best time—"

"You think?"

"But I'm asking you to be my wife. Will you do me the honour?"

"I... Listen, you get that sword out of here, and when I meet up with you again, I'll give you my answer, OK?"

"OK," he said. "OK. I love you."

The ground crumbled as he sank down into it, and a moment later, Vex and Saracen came sprinting down the corridor – the vampire right behind them.

"Aw, hell," breathed Tanith.

Vex and Saracen ran by. Tanith jumped to the ceiling and sprinted along with them. They rounded a corner, kept going.

"Either of you have a plan?" she asked from above.

Saracen was too busy panting for breath to answer. He used to be so much fitter. Vex, on the other hand, didn't seem bothered by how fast he was moving.

"Let's split up," he said, raising his eyes to look at her. "We'll keep running this way, you stop running completely. It's the last thing it'll expect. Hopefully, the shock will lead to a heart attack or something."

"Or," Saracen gasped, "we can run into a room and... Tanith can... seal the door behind us."

"The simpler option," Vex conceded. "OK, let's do that, then."

Tanith flipped to the ground as Vex and Saracen burst into some kind of conference room. She darted in after them, turned as they slammed the double doors shut. She pressed her hand to the wood, but the vampire collided with the doors from the other side, throwing them open, knocking Tanith to the ground. The vampire dived for her, but a blast of energy sent it spinning away.

Tanith scrambled up, lunged out into the corridor, tried shutting the doors to lock Vex and Saracen in there with the vampire, but Vex got his hand in the gap.

"Ow," he growled, opening the doors wide enough so that he and Saracen could slip out.

"Oh, good," Tanith said. "You made it..."

The doors closed and she pressed her hand to the wood and a sheen spread. The vampire hit the doors from the other side, but they didn't even rattle.

"What do you know?" she said. "We actually make a good team."

Saracen went low and Vex went high, and they brought her down and pinned her to the ground. She tried to push them off, but Vex grabbed her wrist and twisted. She struggled until she felt the cold steel of a handcuff and heard it click behind her.

Immediately her strength faded and her magic dimmed. Vex pulled her right arm back, cuffing it to the left. Saracen took her sword away before he stood, and Vex took hold of her arm and helped her to her feet.

"Tanith Low," he said, "you're under arrest."

"You're really putting a dampener on the high spirits here, Dexter."

"Sorry about that." With Tanith between them, they walked back the way they'd come. The alarms, she realised, had been shut off. There were no sounds of fighting. She didn't care about that. The only thing she cared about was that Sanguine had managed to get away with the God-Killer. The only thing that mattered was destroying those weapons.

"If you're lucky," said Vex, "they'll agree to let you serve your time in Ireland. I know Ghastly wants to do everything he can to help you."

"I'm beyond help," she said. "The sooner he accepts that, the better off he'll be."

"You found her," Graves said, walking towards them with a squad of Cleavers behind him. "Excellent."

Two Cleavers came forward, gripped her arms and moved her away from Vex.

"She needs medical attention," Saracen said. "And we'd like to request at this point that she be allowed to serve her sentence in an Irish gaol, where our doctors can work at separating her from the Remnant."

"She's an English sorcerer arrested on English soil," Graves said. "She'll spend the rest of her life rotting in an English cell, thank you very much. And speaking of rotting in cells..."

The Cleavers seized Vex and Saracen.

Saracen twisted, tried to pull away. "What the hell are you doing?"

"We broke in here," Vex reminded him.

"Oh," said Saracen, "yeah," and allowed himself to be shackled.

Tanith looked at the pair of them. "Happy?" she asked. "Now we're all in chains. We could have all run, but no. You had to be the good guys."

"It's what we are," said Vex.

"You're idiots."

"That's what we are, too," said Saracen, a little sadly.

27

he cell door opened and a Cleaver beckoned. Vex stood up stiffly. They'd taken his pouch of leaves away from him, and his leg was hurting like hell. He was led, limping, to the Great Chamber. The others were already here, standing before three empty podiums. Saracen and Frightening looked none the worse for wear, but Gracious and Donegan were sporting spectacular bruises and Aurora was holding her side, in obvious pain.

The podiums slid open and thrones rose up. Flashy. Seated in those thrones were Elders Palaver Graves and Illori Reticent, a pretty woman who wore a permanently bored expression on her face. Occupying the middle throne was Grand Mage Cothernus Ode. He was handsome but lined, the years having long since taken their toll on his skin. His white hair was cut tight to his scalp and he wore his Elder's robes like an afterthought. He was as fierce as he was intelligent, and he was not a man to be underestimated.

Ode was reading from a piece of paper as the thrones settled into place with a click. He took another few moments before finally raising his eyes.

"Grand Mage Ravel is insisting you be released," he said, sounding amused. "I've explained to him, repeatedly, that you entered this Sanctuary illegally, assaulting a member of my staff as you did so, with the intention of stealing a valuable and dangerous weapon. We would be quite within our rights to throw you in the nearest gaol and forget about you."

Vex stood there with the others, said nothing.

"The fact, however, that you were breaking our laws in order to stop Tanith Low and her cohorts does show you in a slightly more favourable light. Only slightly, mind you. But enough to possibly get you a reduced sentence... if we were feeling lenient." Ode paused, long enough to glance at Graves with disapproval. "But on viewing the footage that was recorded during this incident, and after speaking to various witnesses, this Council is ready to admit that your actions saved some lives – not least of which

Elder Graves's. You could have used the chaos to make your escape, but you didn't. You stayed and helped and... we appreciate that."

"You're welcome," said Saracen. Vex saw Aurora kick his ankle to shut him up.

"And so," said Ode, "you are to be released without charge. If, however, you are seen in England any time over the next three years without written permission from this Council, you will be rearrested. Do I make myself clear?"

"What about Tanith?" Vex asked.

Ode looked at him coolly. "What about her, Mr Vex?"

"The Irish Sanctuary has Dr Nye ready and waiting to help her. If anyone can separate her from the Remnant, Nye is the creature to do it."

"Nye," said Ode. "Nye... where have I heard that name? Oh, yes, I remember. On the lips of all the prisoners it tortured to death, that's where. The Irish Sanctuary is harbouring a war criminal responsible for the deaths of—"

"They're harbouring no one," Frightening cut in. "The terms of the Treaty afforded an amnesty to Nye as much as it did to anyone else who fought on Mevolent's side."

"You're defending a war criminal?"

"I'm defending the Irish Sanctuary."

"Be careful where you place your allegiances, Mr Jones," said

Ode. "And the same can be said for your fellow sorcerers in the African Sanctuaries. It might not be a good idea to side with a volatile Sanctuary that is so increasingly isolated."

"That sounds vaguely like a threat," said Frightening.

"Excuse me," Gracious said, offering up a smile, "if it might be possible to just go back to the bit where you're offering us a grudging thanks and letting us get away with breaking in here, that'd be absolutely wonderful."

Ode grunted. "Yes, well, perhaps it would be best if we cut this conversation short. Mr Vex, Tanith Low is staying here as our prisoner, as is Wilhelm Scream. The body of Black Annis will be cremated and her ashes buried in an unmarked grave. As for the vampire..."

A man came forward and spoke into Ode's ear. Ode grunted again, and waved him away. "The vampire has so far eluded us."

"Eluded you?" Aurora echoed. "But it's morning. The sun is up. Dusk would have regrown his skin by now."

"I understand that."

"Grand Mage Ode, you're looking for a naked man running around the Sanctuary. How can he go unnoticed?"

"I have my top people working on it right now."

"Who?"

He glared at her. "Top. People. You should all take a leaf from

Mr O'Callahan's book, by the way. He sees the sense in not antagonising the person who is showing him mercy."

"Also, I have to pee," said Gracious.

"Out," Ode said, sighing. "All of you. Out. Do not darken my doorstep again."

All of which left only one more thing to do – and it was not something Vex was looking forward to.

He said his farewells to the others, thanking them for their help in what had turned out to be a complete disaster of a mission, and then he returned to Ireland. There was a car waiting for him at the airport to take him straight to Roarhaven. He knocked on Ghastly Bespoke's door and entered.

Ghastly was hurling fists into the punchbag in the corner of his office. With the ferocity he was putting into the shots, Vex was pretty sure he knew who he was thinking about.

"Why didn't you tell me?" Ghastly asked without even looking at him. His scarred face was covered in a light sheen of sweat.

"Because you'd have wanted to come along with us," said Vex, "and you can't do that any more. You're an Elder. You have to stay behind."

Ghastly moved round the bag, tapping out a succession of jabs. "This is Tanith we're talking about."

"Exactly." Vex perched on the edge of the desk to take the

weight off his injured leg. "It's personal. You can't afford to let things get personal. Sorry, Ghastly, there was no way I was telling you."

"That was a mistake. That was a huge..." Ghastly hit the bag with a right hook and the whole frame shuddered. Now he looked at Vex as he took off his gloves. "We'd have been able to organise back-up. You'd have had all the resources you'd need. We could have got this done quick and clean and we'd have the God-Killers *and* we'd have Tanith."

"No. It wouldn't have worked. Tanith's involvement meant that it never had a *chance* of working. Because of her, we were discovered by both the German and the English Sanctuaries. The only reason we're not at war right now is because you had no idea what I was planning."

Ghastly grabbed a towel, wiped himself down. "Where is she now? Is she still in London? We can get her transferred over—"

"I tried. Ode isn't having it."

"Well, he can at least have his doctors try and get the Remnant out of her."

"He's not interested in saving her – just punishing her. And, by extension, you. Listen, Ghastly, when all this is over, when both sides have calmed down and things are back to normal, he'll transfer her. You know he will. Until then, she's in a prison cell."

Ghastly let out a long, slow breath. "Yeah. At least she's safe, I suppose. She can't hurt anyone. No one can hurt her. What about the God-Killers?"

"From what we can gather, they're in the possession of Billy-Ray Sanguine, who apparently has strict orders to destroy them. For Tanith, this was all about preventing their use against Darquesse – she never had any plans to use them herself."

"But now that she's been captured, Sanguine might hold on to them," said Ghastly. "We should concentrate on tracking him down."

"With the primary goal being the recovery of the God-Killers," said Vex, "or the beating up of Billy-Ray?"

Ghastly shrugged. "We can't do both?"

Vex let himself smile for a moment. "Darquesse is being forgotten about," he said. "The attention of every Council around the world is focused here. All anyone is talking about are the rising tensions and this war that everyone's assuming is an inevitability. We've taken our eye off the ball, Ghastly. When Darquesse comes, she's going to take us by surprise, no matter how much warning we've been given."

"Then it's a good thing we have people like you and Skulduggery and Valkyrie, isn't it?" Ghastly said. "People who can ignore orders and protocol and just do what needs to be done."

Vex raised an eyebrow. "Is that your way of giving me permission to keep doing what I'm doing?"

"Since when do you need permission? Just try not to actually *start* this war, OK? We're in enough trouble as it is. How's Saracen, by the way?"

"Same as ever. He says hi. Told me to tell you if the Council of Elders needs him, just call."

"We were planning on it. You found out what his power is yet?"

Vex scowled. "No, I didn't. But I will."

28

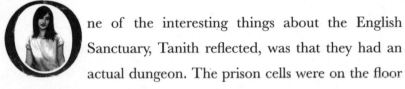ne of the interesting things about the English Sanctuary, Tanith reflected, was that they had an actual dungeon. The prison cells were on the floor above, with their clean lines and sanitary conditions, but the dungeon was where the real magic happened, as it were, with the bars and straw on the floor and chains on the walls. It was all dark and lit by flaming torches. All very Gothic. All very moody. All very London.

The wardens of this delightful place were an odd pair. A handsome fat man and an ugly skinny man who only stopped bickering long enough to debate on whether they should hang

Tanith upside down on the wall. The consensus reached was that she was a Wall-Walker, and so she'd probably be quite used to hanging upside down, so really what would be the point?

So here she stood, arms shackled above her head, alone in the dark and the cold once again. She didn't care. The important thing was that by now Sanguine would have taken the God-Killers to the furnace and melted them all down. The important thing was that Darquesse was now safe. Tanith smiled. Then she looked around. God this was boring.

Someone approached and looked in through the bars at her. He didn't fling ill-conceived insults, so it wasn't either of the wardens. He stepped into the light and she met his eyes, but her defiance quickly turned to curiosity.

"I know you," Tanith said. "I saw you in Germany. At the party."

"Indeed you did," said the dark-haired man.

"Who are you?"

"My name is Moribund."

"Moribund," she said. "From where do I know that name?"

"I was a prisoner," said the man, "in Dublin. I was held in a cage, and you released me."

"So that was *you*... Forgive me for not recognising you immediately – I'd just been stabbed and my mind was on other things. I got into a little bit of trouble for that, you know. I explained that I was not in control of my actions, but when Thurid Guild took over, he was all set to throw me in a cell for helping a known murderer escape."

"He didn't, though."

"Mr Bliss convinced him I was telling the truth."

"A good man, that Mr Bliss. Terrible what happened to him."

Tanith laughed. "You know, the regret in your voice would almost be believable if I hadn't read your file."

Moribund smiled sadly. There was something under his arm, something long and wrapped in cloth. "And what did it say, this file?"

"From what I can remember, you started out as just another sorcerer, though probably a humourless one, judging by your name... And then you turned into a sadistic psychopath and killer."

"That's all?"

"It was a few years ago. I may have forgotten some details. So what's a humourless, sadistic psychopath and escaped convict doing working for the English Sanctuary?"

"I don't work for them," said Moribund. "I broke in here, the same as you."

"Why?"

"To help, of course."

She frowned. "To help me?"

"I owed you a favour. When you released me, I went into hiding. I didn't hurt anyone, I didn't kill anyone. Ever so slowly, I started building a new life for myself. It was small and humble, but it was my own."

"Good for you."

"And then I heard that a Remnant had bonded with you, and I knew that if ever you needed a favour repaid, it would be now. So I found you. And helped you."

"You helped me? How, exactly, did you help me?"

"Two men with guns waiting for you in Chicago. Another with a sniper rifle that you never even saw."

"That was you?"

"And then, while you fought Crab on that beach in Poland, two Sanctuary agents about to call in your position."

"You're my guardian angel?"

"I'm no angel. I had avoided the use of violence for the last five years. It has been... distressing how easily I can slip back into my old ways."

"And now you're here to get me out, right?"

"Of course."

Keys rattled in the lock and the door swung wide. He picked another key from the collection in his hand as he came forward, and a moment later, Tanith's shackles sprang open. While she rubbed her wrists, he unwrapped the bundle of cloth, and handed over her sword in its black scabbard.

"I liberated this on my way here," he said. "I thought it might hold some sentimental value."

"It does," Tanith said. "Did you know that Valkyrie Cain used this sword to kill the Grotesquery? That was the first time she ever saved the world. Wasn't the last."

They walked from the cell, and Tanith sighed as she felt her magic flood back into her body. They passed the wardens slumped on the ground.

"Dead?" she asked.

"Unconscious," Moribund said. "I do not kill if it can be avoided. You don't have to, either, you know."

"I'm grateful for the rescue, but if you're going to start lecturing me..."

"And what if the lecture *is* the rescue? Releasing your physical form is easy – setting your spirit free is much more difficult."

"Oh, man," said Tanith, "you're not religious, are you?"

He led the way up the stairs. They passed another unconscious man. "Would you hold it against me if I were? But this isn't about religion. When I talk about your spirit, I'm not talking about some elusive idea, I'm talking about your actual soul, which the Remnant has grafted itself on to."

"Well, let me save you the time and the effort. The Remnant's a part of me now and it can't be removed."

"That's quite true."

"OK then."

"But that doesn't mean you have to change who you once were."

"Uh, yes, it does."

Out in the corridor now, Moribund was walking with the confidence of one who knows he will not be discovered. Tanith stuck close to him.

"The Remnant erases your conscience and removes your ability to empathise," Moribund said. "It turns you into a sociopath. It also affects other aspects of your personality, but none to any significant degree. You are still, essentially, who you have always been."

"What are you, a Remnant expert?"

"Yes," said Moribund. "But you can relearn the skills you need to empathise, and you can fake a conscience until it becomes a natural part of you."

"Fake it till you make it, you mean."

"Precisely."

"And what's the point of all that? I'd just be lying to myself."

"The alternative is to surrender and let the Remnant win. Tanith, you have an opportunity to atone for your sins. It's not too late to turn back. You have friends who love you and who would be willing to give you another chance."

She laughed as they climbed another set of stairs. "Moribund, all this is wonderfully inspiring stuff, it really is, but I'm a Remnant, and I want the world to die. I've seen a vision of how it happens and everything I've been doing, collecting all these weapons, is designed to help that along. When she arrives, Darquesse is going to burn this planet to a cinder and I'm ensuring that there are no God-Killer level weapons around to stop her. My old friends aren't going to give me another chance because we're not on the same side any more. Do you get that?"

"Why do you want her to destroy the world?"

"Because I've seen it, and I've never seen anything so beautiful. You wouldn't understand. I've tried explaining it to Billy-Ray and he says he understands, but he doesn't."

"*I* understand."

"No. You don't."

"Yes," Moribund said, turning to her, "I do." Dark veins spread beneath his skin and his lips turned black.

Tanith fell against the wall and stared, her mouth open.

"This is why I went from being a normal, humourless sorcerer to a sadistic psychopath and killer," Moribund said. "A Remnant found me, climbed down my throat, and it's been living inside me ever since. It is as much a part of me now as my own heart or my earliest memory."

"I thought... I thought all the others were trapped."

"All those darting black shadow-creatures are trapped, yes, and some like us, bonded pairs, are in gaols. But there are yet others out there, around the world. Some are bonded to sorcerers, some to mortals, some to other... beings."

"Where are they? Why don't they do something to free the thousands of Remnants who are being kept in the Soul Catcher?"

Moribund smiled. "Because they're sociopaths, Tanith. And the longer they've been bonded, the less they care. It takes a concerted effort to start rebuilding that part of your personality after decades of neglect. For me, it was difficult, bordering on impossible. For you, it will be hard... but within your reach."

"You wouldn't be saying that if you had seen what I saw. It was beautiful."

"I would wager that what you find beautiful is not the same as what I find beautiful. Once, I would have been at your side. But not now."

They walked into the storeroom.

"You can come out," Moribund said.

Wilhelm stood up from behind a crate. He was pale and sweating and his hand was heavily bandaged, and he looked at Tanith like she had just kicked his puppy. "You cut off my finger."

"Yes," she said. "I remember."

"But I was on your team!"

"Because I needed to cut off your finger."

"But—"

"Wilhelm. I cut off your finger because that's what I needed to do. I didn't tell you about it because I didn't think you'd be too keen on the idea. With all your blubbering, and with your tone of voice now, I see that I was right. But we did what we came here to do, and I really don't see what your problem is."

Wilhelm gaped at her.

"I'm sorry," said Moribund. "Should I not have released Mr Scream also?"

"Naw, it's fine," said Tanith. "He's just feeling emotional. Do you know how to get us out of here?"

Moribund nodded. "I watched Mr Chabon let you in. Face the wall. You, too, Mr Scream."

Wilhelm hurried over and stood beside Tanith. He glanced at the sword on her back, then glared at her. "Be careful you don't cut off another one of my—"

"Be quiet," Tanith said.

Wilhelm shut up.

The bright light flowed over them and Tanith felt her body tingle. She stepped forward, through the wall, emerging into the morning air. The smell of freedom.

Wilhelm scowled at her. "Next time you assemble a team," he said, "be sure to leave me—"

"They're going to notice we're not in our cells any moment now, Wilhelm. You don't have time to make a parting quip, even if you could think of one."

His lower lip trembled, and he spun and ran.

"What a strange little man," Moribund said. The veins were gone from his face as he looked back at Tanith. "Think about what I said."

"That's it? You're just going to walk off?"

"You helped me escape, and I've returned the favour. Now that we're even, I have my life to get back to."

"But we both have Remnants inside us. Shouldn't we, you know, stick together?"

"Why would we? I don't limit myself because of what I am," he said as he walked away. "Do you?"

Figuring that pretty soon the rooftops would be covered with Cleavers searching for her, Tanith took a cab. She sat there with her sword across her lap and her coat over it and talked to the driver about famous people he'd had in his back seat. She hadn't heard of most of them. *Carry On My Wayward Son* came on the radio and they sang along with it.

She got out a mile from her destination and walked the rest

of the way, making sure she wasn't being followed. The building had once been a blacksmith's all those years before. It still had a working furnace, and she felt the heat the moment she slipped in through the window. It was dark and still, like the whole place was holding its breath.

Movement behind her and she whirled and Sanguine wrapped her in his arms. "I thought I'd never see you again."

She waited until he was done, then stepped away and gave him a smile. "I'm just glad you managed to get away from those things under the Sanctuary," she said. "Did you find out what they were?"

He shook his head. "And I didn't wait around to ask questions, either. I ain't gonna lie – whatever they are, they worry me. I've never heard of anything like it."

"Well," Tanith said, having wasted enough time on small talk, "the good news is, we both got out, we're both free and the weapons have been destroyed, right?"

He nodded, then made a face. "Half of 'em, yeah."

She stared. "What?"

"I melted down the sword and the spear," he said. "But I figured I might have to go back in there to rescue you, and having the bow and the dagger might not be a bad idea."

"I told you to destroy *all* the weapons!"

"Hey, calm down, OK? I was just taking precautions."

"I didn't ask you to take precautions," she said, walking past him, "I told you to melt them all down."

He caught up to her. "Would you please relax? I kept the furnace going so that if I saw anything suspicious, I could just throw 'em in."

Tanith ignored him. The furnace room blasted heat at her when she entered. There they were, the bow and the dagger, sitting out in plain view. She picked up the blade, felt its power, felt how even the tiniest of nicks would open Sanguine up and spread his insides across the floor.

Instead, she threw the dagger into the furnace, then pushed the bow in after it. She glared.

"OK," Sanguine said, "you're mad at me."

"If they had followed you back here," Tanith said, "they could have recovered these before you had a chance to destroy them. Then everything we'd done would have been for nothing, and when Darquesse appeared, they'd be ready for her."

"It was a precaution," he said. "That's all. And look, all destroyed now. All melted down. Problem solved."

"You risked everything for nothing."

"I risked everything for *you*."

"You shouldn't have done that."

He went to hug her but she slapped his hands away.

He sighed, scratched his jaw. "Listen to me. All you care about is Darquesse, right? But me? All I care about is you. You understand? You are my Darquesse. You'd do anything for her, and I'd do anything for you."

"But I don't matter. Only she matters."

"You matter to me. We can argue about this all day if you want, and that's OK. I can do that. But it ain't gonna change the fact that I love you."

"Billy-Ray... the only reason I'm with you is because of this Remnant inside me."

"I know that."

"You say you love me, but you're a sociopath just like I am. You're incapable of love."

"That's what they say. But I don't believe it. This thing I'm feeling, I'm pretty sure that's love. It makes me crazy, makes me stupid, makes me ornery as all hell, but now that I have it I never want to let it go."

"Even though you know I can never return those feelings?"

He smiled. "Never say never, sword-lady. The power of love has allowed me to transcend my psychopathic nature. Maybe you can transcend whatever limitations people put on you as well."

She couldn't help it, she had to smile. "For a cold-blooded killer, you're remarkably romantic."

His arms wrapped round her. "You get the full Billy-Ray Sanguine experience, my darlin'." He kissed her and she kissed him back. "So... had any thoughts on what we were talking about before?"

She looked at him blankly for a moment. His proposal. She'd forgotten all about it. Before she could answer, though, he tensed. She turned slowly.

"I was wondering where you'd got to," she said.

Dusk looked at them both, but said nothing.

"Listen," Tanith said, "if you're going to gripe about how I left you to fend for yourself—"

"Not at all," said Dusk. "We must each take responsibility for ourselves. Besides, there is nothing you could have done to contain me."

"Well," Tanith said, "I'm glad you see it like that. By the way, I've got some fresh wounds on my back courtesy of you."

"Such is the price we pay for the things we do. Others have paid an even higher price, I have heard. You cut Wilhelm Scream's hand off?"

"Just his finger."

"I see. Annis is dead, of course. Sabine, too, I'd wager, after you betrayed her to that man Chabon. And Springheeled Jack? What happened to him?"

"I did," said Tanith.

Dusk nodded. Out of the corner of her eye, Tanith saw Sanguine's hand inch towards his pocket, where he kept the straight razor.

"You have betrayed almost half the members of your little team," the vampire said. "And what, may I ask, of the rewards you promised them?"

Tanith shrugged. "I promised Annis a cure for her curse. I didn't have one. I promised Jack information on what he was and where he came from. No one knows where he came from. There have been reports of creatures like him centuries ago, but that's it. I promised Sabine a way to wipe her slate clean, to start a new life where she didn't have to look over her shoulder every five minutes. I had no intention of doing any such thing."

"And you promised me the name of the vampire who turned me," said Dusk. "A name you do not possess, I take it?"

"Actually," Tanith said, "I do. The survivors get their rewards, Dusk. Wilhelm gets his, and you get yours. Besides, I make it a rule never to give a vampire a reason to hold a grudge."

"And this name?"

Tanith smiled at him. "Moloch."

Dusk's eyes narrowed. "You're lying."

"I'm not."

"I've known Moloch for centuries. We have never liked each other, but he has never given any indication that he was the one who ended my mortal life."

"I doubt he even knows," Tanith said. "Do *you* remember every single detail of what *you* do when you change? I'd say it gets quite confusing in that little head of yours. From what I read, he had only been a vampire for a few years himself before he came to that town. I'm telling you the truth, Dusk. What you do with it now is up to you."

"If I find out you're lying..."

She laughed. "Lying to you would be bad for my health."

Dusk kept his eyes on her for a bit, and then left.

"Phew," said Sanguine, visibly relaxing. "Thought that was gonna get nasty for a moment. That true, by the way? About Moloch?"

"That was the name in the report," she said as she turned back to him. "You know something, Billy-Ray? You're a very useful person to have by my side. I can't think of anyone I'd rather have. I don't know what I'd do without you."

His hands found her hips and he pulled her closer. "Does that mean you'll marry me?"

"You know I can't love you back, right?"

"Not yet you can't. And I'm OK with that."

"Then, yes. I'll marry you."

Sanguine gave her the widest smile she'd ever seen him give, and he kissed her and she kissed him.

29

It wasn't easy, lying to Tanith.

He didn't like doing it, that's for sure. He loved her. He'd finally found someone to love, someone as mixed up and messed up as he was, and he wasn't about to let her go. No, sir. He knew a good thing when he found it and he was no fool.

But Sanguine, well, above all else he was a pragmatic son of a gun, and he reckoned that there wasn't a whole lot of point in helping someone you love bring about the end of the world if the end of the world meant you couldn't be with the one you love. So he'd had Sabine use her mojo to charge up another set of dummy weapons. If they could fool the so-called experts for a few days, he saw no reason why they couldn't fool Tanith for a few minutes as she watched them melt. He'd felt bad about it. The look on her face as she stood there, that smile that opened up, it was almost enough to make him confess, to make him tell her about the real weapons that he'd hidden away.

Almost. But not quite. Sanguine was in love. But that didn't make him stupid. And now that he had access to some of the most powerful weapons in the world, well... that pretty much made him even more of a badass.

And, when you got down to it, pretty goddamn unstoppable.

Skulduggery Pleasant.

Need a little more *magic* in your life?

Join the Skulduggery Pleasant mailing list
and keep bang up to date with everything
that's going on in the world of Skulduggery!

Plus, if you register now, you could
WIN exclusive Skulduggery prizes...

www.skulduggerypleasant.co.uk/comp

The dead famous bestsellers:
out now in paperback